OPPOSITE ATTRACTION
THE KELLER FAMILY SERIES
BOOK THREE

BERNADETTE MARIE

5 PRINCE PUBLISHING AND BOOKS, LLC

PO Box 865, Arvada, CO 80001

www.5PrinceBooks.com

ISBN Digital 978-1-45247-580-6

ISBN Print 978-1-63112-022-0

Opposite Attraction

Copyright Bernadette Marie 2012 -2023

Published by 5 Prince Publishing

Photo Credit: Getty Images

First Edition/First Printing August 2012 Printed U.S.A.

RM07112023

For Stan
No two are more opposite than we—and yet we have perfection!

ACKNOWLEDGMENTS

An enormous thank you to my husband and my boys, thank you for letting me work around all your noise. You feed me in so many ways. It is easy to write about great families because I have one.

To my parents and my sister, thank you for loving me and always believing in me.

To Connie, thank you for keeping me on track, for cheering me on, for patting me on the back, and for just being you.

To Kim, thank you for taking on this project for me, you were a savior in a time of need.

To Amanda, thank you for taking that painstaking job of beta reading this book so I would know if it was readable. Your kind words and remarks were invaluable!

To my beloved readers, thank you for supporting me and my passion for writing for you. Each of you brightens my days and makes my job easy.

ALSO BY BERNADETTE MARIE

THE ROM COM MOVIE CLUB

The Rom Com Movie Club - Book One

The Rom Com Movie Club - Book Two

The Rom Com Movie Club - Book Three

FUNERALS AND WEDDINGS SERIES

Something Lost

Something Discovered

Something Found

Something Forbidden

Something New

THE DEVEREAUX FAMILY SERIES

Kennedy Devereaux

Chase Devereaux

Max Devereaux

Paige Devereaux

STANDALONE TITLES

The Happily Ever After Bookstore

Liz's Road Trip

THE MATCHMAKER SERIES

Matchmakers

Encore

Finding Hope

THE THREE MRS. MONROES TRILOGY

Amelia

Penelope

Vivian

OPPOSITE ATTRACTION

CHAPTER 1

*C*hampagne flowed, again.

His brother had married, again.

Curtis Keller knew this marriage would last, this time, but he wondered if he'd ever love again.

He sipped from his glass and watched his brother, Carlos, dance with the only woman he'd ever truly loved. His Madeline.

Curtis leaned up against the pillar of his sister Regan's porch and watched as couples danced with the bride and groom in the garden. He gave a little chuckle to himself. Carlos and Madeline had been young when they'd first married. No one ever saw it coming, the day Carlos announced that he and Madeline were getting divorced.

She'd gone on and remarried. It had taken Carlos five years to finally remarry, but that had lasted less than a day. Now here they all were celebrating their second marriage, to each other.

Curtis tipped his glass in a toast when Madeline glanced his way. She was a glorious sight, and as a doctor, as well as her dear friend, he was happy for her. Only a year earlier she'd been diagnosed with breast cancer. But with a full head of chestnut hair swinging at her shoulders, compliments of his sister

Arianna's extensive wig collection, no one would have ever known that only months earlier Carlos had shaved off all of her natural hair.

His nephews and niece danced among them. His brother-in-law, Zach, danced with his own mother and Curtis' parents hadn't missed a song all night. In the middle of the dance floor was his older sister, Arianna, and her date from Carlos' last wedding, and Zach's right hand man in his construction company, John Forrester. They seemed comfortable, as comfortable as you could be with a set-up-date.

As for him, he was happy to watch. The memory of his date at Carlos' last wedding, still burned in his gut. Tonight he didn't have an escort, and that was just how he wanted it.

His sister Regan slid up next to him, a glass of champagne in her hand. "You look lost in thought."

He scanned a look over her. "Are you supposed to be drinking that?"

"I won't tell if you don't."

He shook his head. "Expectant mothers aren't supposed to drink."

She nudged him. "Well the expectant father said I could have just a little sip, and since the expectant brother is sleeping, I'm not going to worry about it." She lifted the glass to her lips and drank the bubbly drink. Curtis grabbed her hand and she laughed. "It's sparkling cider. I made sure we had plenty for the kids." She laughed as Curtis settled back against the pillar.

Regan was a wonder to him. There she stood a happy woman married to the man of her dreams. Their son was almost a year old and she was weeks into her second pregnancy. Only he and her husband Zach knew about the baby. She was waiting until after the wedding to announce that she was expecting. She hadn't wanted to take away from the celebration happening around them.

Regan shifted her glance from the dance floor back to him. "You don't seem to be having as much fun at this wedding."

"You didn't arrange a date for me this time either."

With a slow nod, Regan sipped from the drink, and then handed him her glass. "I'm going to go steal my husband away from his mother."

Curtis watched her do just that and he retreated to the kitchen before Zach's mother, Audrey, caught him and begged him to dance.

Caterers moved about the house and Curtis fixed himself a plate of fruit. He'd be happier in the kitchen he decided. The reception was depressing him.

When he lifted his head from the platters of food, he saw the reason it depressed him standing right in front of him.

"Hello, Curtis." Simone Pierpont's French accent stabbed right into his heart before he choked on the grape he'd just swallowed whole.

He coughed until he could breathe. Her eyes never wavered from him and he was sure they had bored a hole right through him.

"Simone. I didn't expect you here."

She twisted her fingers together and smiled nervously. "I've been out of town."

Didn't he know that? He'd tried for the past two months to find her. Even his brother-in-law, Zach, who she claimed was her very dearest friend, hadn't known where to find her.

"You're looking well." He wasn't sure what else to say. He'd been dumped by women before, but it had never hurt like this one did. Oh, she'd had him fooled. Yes, he thought there'd been a chance for something real. He'd thought it was love.

But he had to acknowledge that there were women in the world who appreciated the art of seduction and fast steamy love affairs without stings just as men did. He just never thought he'd be the man who was used and disposed of.

3

Damn her anyway, he thought.

She took a step toward him and then stopped just short of reaching him. Her knuckles were white now and her nervousness wasn't helping him keep calm.

Simone bit down on her lip then shifted her blue eyes to his. "I would have called..."

"Listen," he set down his plate. "You don't owe me any explanations. Zach and Regan set us up to share the evening together so we wouldn't be alone. They didn't tell us to," he lowered his voice, "screw like rabbits and run off to your yacht in the French Riviera. So we had a good time. Really, who thought much of it?" He had and he fought his eyes to make sure she didn't know how much he'd thought of it.

"Right. It was just sex. I was hoping you would understand that."

"Got it." He picked up his plate. "Well I think I'll go see how the party is going. See ya 'round."

CHAPTER 2

*T*hat wasn't exactly how Simone had hoped that would go. She untangled her fingers realizing they were almost numb now.

Curtis deserved to treat her like that. She'd been very forthcoming with him, over too much champagne on her yacht, that she'd bedded many men. Why she felt he needed to know that, she wasn't sure. She'd left out the hefty part of the tale though. Most of those men had been in her bed while she tried to wrap her head around the fact that Zachary Benson, Curtis' brother-in-law, had never seen her as more than a sister or dear friend.

Lucky for her, she loved him the same. She was glad he and Regan had found each other and now had a family. But that hadn't changed her view on herself. Simone Pierpont longed for what Zach now had. Love, marriage, and a family. One piece didn't really fit without the other.

She sucked in a breath. Had she not made such an ass out of herself in front of Curtis, and then run off without a word, stranding him on the Rivera to find his own way home, perhaps she'd have just that.

Simone ran her hands over the slim satin line of her dress, lingering only a moment on her jittery stomach.

Well, she thought, at least she'd have some of what Zach had.

CURTIS LIFTED A GLASS OF CHAMPAGNE FROM THE TRAY AS HE walked out into the garden. He drank it down fast, the bubbles shooting straight into his head. As another waiter passed, he set it down and lifted another. He wasn't on call at the hospital for another two days, he'd surely be fine with a few more glasses, especially now that Simone Pierpont had joined the party.

She'd made her way out of the house he noticed. She stood wrapped in his brother-in-law's arms as his own sister looked on lovingly. What an idiot he'd been thinking that it was wise to have whisked her away that night. They'd taken their first tumble right there behind the house.

He drank down that glass of champagne. In all his life, that hadn't been his style. What in the hell had he been thinking?

There lay the problem. He hadn't been thinking. Not with his head anyway. He hadn't even realized his brother had been dumped the next morning by his new wife and sent off to find his ex-wife. No, he'd fled the country on that damned lovely yacht with a near perfect woman only to come home and find his brother cuddled on his mother's couch with the woman he'd once been married to. Talk about a shock to the system.

He knew there was trouble headed his way when he saw all three of them shift their heads and look at him. Quickly, he finished the glass of champagne and blew out a breath as he tried to focus on Zach walking to him. Things were becoming a bit fuzzy.

"Regan wants me to go in and check on Tyler. Why don't you walk with me."

It wasn't an invitation, Curtis realized, but a request. He followed Zach up the stairs to the small room where his nephew slept. Zach poked his head in and came back with a smile.

"She's a bit paranoid with all these people here, but he's fine."

"Good," Curtis said quickly and turned for his retreat.

"Why don't we go down to the study and have a drink." Zach walked down the stairs and Curtis reluctantly followed. He wasn't sure another drink was a good idea, and when Zach shut the door he wasn't sure being in the same room with the man was either.

Zach moved to the liquor cabinet and pulled open the doors. "I got a new bottle of whiskey last week from Ireland. A business associate sent it to me. What do you say?"

Curtis swallowed the words he really was thinking and gave his brother-in-law a nod.

Zach poured them each two fingers full and handed Curtis a sniffer.

"To Carlos and Madeline."

"To them," Curtis said as he threw back his drink and then blew out a fiery breath. Certainly, it was going to take the next two days off work to sober up.

"Good stuff." Zach looked in his glass. "Want another?"

"No." That came out quickly enough he thought. He needed to sit, but Zach was walking around the room as if he needed to talk. Curtis tried to hold on to the ground with his feet firmly planted, but the room was beginning to tilt.

Zach sat on the edge of his desk. "I was surprised to see Simone here tonight, weren't you?"

Curtis shrugged. "Your house. Your friend."

"She sure is. My dearest friend in the world." Zach nodded and then turned his eyes up to him. "She seems a little nervous to be here. She's never been nervous."

He shrugged again, but when his shoulders fell he decided he needed to make it to the couch before the room completely spun on him. "Maybe she's uneasy being here for another of Carlos' weddings." The thought made him laugh. Two weddings in two months, was that a record or something?

Zach moved to the seat across from the couch where he'd landed and sat down. "It seems to us she's a little uneasy being around you."

In his current state, Curtis took that as an insult. It was fine if his sister and his brother-in-law thought more of some rich French girl than they did of him. Him, who saved lives every single day. Him, who on occasion, had been known to save his own sister's life, but that wasn't something anyone talked about anymore. Hell, he should be put on a back burner just because of the sexy, leggy, raven haired, blue eyed goddess who seemed to always show up unannounced. He completely understood why *her* uneasiness was a problem.

No, no he didn't.

He tried to focus his eyes. How many glasses of champagne had he had before the whisky? Oh wait—with more thought, he, Carlos, and Zach had already had a few shots before the wedding. No wonder he couldn't focus.

Zach sat back in his seat. "So what went on between the two of you? Simone has never said, and Regan and I have only speculated."

Speculated? Who was Zach kidding? They'd disappeared together for two weeks. Even the hospital was *speculating* if he'd return.

Never in Curtis Keller's entire life had he blown off responsibility as he had with Simone, but damn it had felt good. It felt good until he woke up on the yacht and she was gone.

The pattern in the carpet was making him dizzy. He looked up and tried desperately to focus on the bow tie of Zach's tuxedo. "I know she's very special to you, but you don't want details."

Zach smiled with a slow nod. "You're right, I don't need details. She is very special." He looked around the room as if to make sure no one was there. "If you don't mind not telling her I said this, she's a bit of a manizer." That seemed to strike Zach as funny and he laughed. "You know, like a womanizer, only a manizer."

"I got it." But it wasn't funny to him. "What about it?"

"Well we were afraid she dug her claws into you."

That would be an understatement as Curtis remembered it. "Don't worry about me. I'm fine."

"Good. She's going to be staying here for a bit and we don't want it to be awkward for you."

Curtis ran his tongue over his teeth and then did it again. His tongue was numb. "I'll be fine. I'll be working lots of shifts at the hospital so I won't be hanging around here too much." At least not anymore.

"You're okay with her?"

"Sure." Why wouldn't he be? No reason to get worked up just because a woman used you for a quick romp. Really, he was more of a man than that.

"Well I'd better get out to the guests. Feel free to hang here and rest your head."

Curtis acknowledged his generosity with a grunt as he tipped his head back on the couch.

CHAPTER 3

The house was quiet when Curtis finally pried open his eyes. Someone had laid a throw over him, Regan no doubt. His head was throbbing and his mouth was desert dry.

Curtis swung his feet to the floor and stood slowly. Perhaps the caterers had left something in the refrigerator. He could do with a sandwich on those senseless little rolls they had served.

He stumbled to the kitchen, swung open the refrigerator and the light illuminated the room. He winced and realized he'd heard a stifled gasp of someone sitting at the table.

Focused on the small figure at the table, he shut the door quickly. "Thought I was alone."

"I was hungry." Her face was coming into focus, but the accent alerted him to who the woman in the dark was. Simone stood and started toward him. "I just came down for a little snack. Can I make you something?"

He'd wanted to laugh as he wondered if she'd ever had to fend for herself in her life. That wasn't fair. Obviously she'd made herself something to eat right there in the kitchen.

"I'm fine. Go finish your snack."

"You are angry with me."

"You think?" He stepped back from Simone as she approached. That expensive perfume, which had tangled with his senses the last time they stood in that kitchen, was playing games with his body again.

"Curtis, I'm sorry. I meant you no harm." She moved closer to him in the dark. *"Mon ami?"*

"Friends? Sure." He turned and reached into the cupboard for a glass. At the sink, he filled it with water and felt it land in his stomach. He hadn't slept on that couch long enough to ward of the drunk he'd put on. "Damn," he said under his breath.

"Are you all right?"

"Just hadn't planned on spending the night on my sister's couch. I wanted to get home."

"I would be happy to give you a ride."

He lifted a brow. "You drove?"

Simone cleared her throat. "You would be pleased to know I have leased a car. I can drive."

"Hmm, well ain't that something."

He thought he knew her well enough that she'd have had a driver waiting in a car for beck and call.

Even in the dark, he saw her straighten. "You think I am just some spoiled brat, do you not?"

"Honey, if the high heeled shoe fits..."

Her hand whizzed through the dark and had he been sober he might have had a chance to block it before it hit his cheek. The sting of it raced through his skin and a curse flew from his lips. "Forget the ride. I'd rather walk home."

"Why did I think you had better manners than this? *Juidiote.*"

She stormed out of the kitchen. If she was going to be around for a while, he'd have a few more chances of pissing her off and that seemed just fine with him. Curtis rubbed at the ache on his cheek.

Well the last thing he needed was for his sister to see him be disrespectful to her houseguest. He'd call a cab. He'd sleep off his drunk and in two days he'd be at the hospital buried in broken bones, cut hands needing stitches, and heart attacks. Suddenly it seemed more appealing than ever.

SIMONE PACED THE FLOOR OF HER BEDROOM. OH, HE'D SET HER OFF and what made her angrier was that she deserved it. Why had she thought things would just fall into place? She had left him stranded on a yacht in the middle of nowhere. She hadn't had the decency to tell him she was leaving or provide him a way home. Zach had to wire him the money to make it back to Tennessee and she'd heard that he was paying dearly for that at the hospital.

She'd used her wealth to treat him like a prince and then banish him like a pauper. Hadn't he made it clear to her that even though most people thought doctors were self-righteous and rich, he wasn't? Hadn't he told he that he spent more time at the hospital than he did in his little, poorly decorated apartment? Those student loans were plenty and paychecks weren't, he'd said.

But she hadn't expected to fall for him.

Simone looked out over the dark garden from her window and sighed. She'd spent so much of her life trying to be in charge she didn't know what to do when she felt the control slip from her heart. The fact that she'd had many men on that very yacht should have kept things in perspective, but they hadn't. Curtis Keller was the only one who had taken care of her on that yacht, and she didn't know how to deal with it.

Sure, many men took care of her. Each of them wanted a piece of what Simone Pierpont could offer them. Curtis Keller asked for nothing.

They'd been thrown together as dates for Carlos' last wedding. They'd met a few times, but once the bubbly started and the music slowed, things changed. She'd changed in his arms that very night and she followed him to that little, rundown apartment he called home, and she'd loved every moment they'd spent there.

Without a bag, she'd worn his shirts around the house. He'd had an extra toothbrush that he'd paid no more than a dollar for that he gave her, and she'd kept. There was no food in the house of a single man and he ordered pizza, and over tipped the driver. It was heaven.

Then she convinced him to run away with her for a few weeks. Leaving behind the responsibility and the woes of saving lives to make love to her on the French Riviera under the stars. And so he did.

And that was where she'd left him.

Simone crawled into bed and pulled the sheets up to her chin as if to hide herself in the dark. She'd never been in a situation where she didn't know what to do or have her daddy to go to fix all her problems. The last time she'd spoken to her father, he'd turned her away, taken away her trust fund, her villa—everything. To him she was nothing, and he'd made that perfectly clear.

It was hard for her to imagine. Her mother had married, again, and lived in Spain. And now Simone couldn't even afford to go to her. Zach had been kind enough to fly her to America and offer her a place to stay. She was sure even Regan didn't know he'd done as much.

Zach didn't know why she was there, but she'd tell him. And Zachary Benson would never turn her away. That was what friends did for each other.

She'd hoped Curtis wouldn't turn her away either, but it didn't look as though things were going her way.

From the book she bought, Simone figured she had a good two months before she needed to make her decisions on matters at hand. Zach offered to help her find a job. Why would she need a job, she supposed he wondered. Suddenly an apartment, dark and dank like Curtis', seemed appealing.

It would all be okay.

She was nearing the end of her thirties and she'd never taken care of herself. She could learn.

The first tear rolled down her cheek and she brushed it away.

People did it all the time.

She was good with math. A budget. She could make a budget. Clothing. She and Regan had once been the same size. Perhaps she could talk her into passing down some of the clothes she had yet to work herself into after Tyler's birth. That would do for a little bit.

She blew out a breath and sucked up the tears that continued. She'd learn to take care of another. People did it all the time.

Simone ran her hands over her belly and swallowed hard. Soon Curtis wouldn't turn her away. At least not completely. But she'd have to prove that she could take care of herself before she told him she was carrying his baby.

CHAPTER 4

*N*ormally, being called into work on his day off wasn't ideal, but Curtis dressed quickly and headed to the hospital.

Since his brother's wedding he'd managed to avoid Simone, and the rest of his family. That had been awkward to say the least when he'd all but ignored his sister's "hello" from the window when he'd picked up his truck out front of her house.

By the time the shift he'd been called in for was over, he'd be onto his own shift. Perhaps she'd be long gone by the time he emerged from the hospital Friday afternoon.

When he was working he lived, breathed, ate, and slept at the hospital. He'd sleep in the room designated for residents and shower there as well. Food wasn't a problem, he'd grown accustomed to hospital food over the years, when there was time to eat. Though he was sure he wouldn't have to worry about eating from the cafeteria. He'd seen the schedule. Nurse Cynthia O'Dell was working the same shift. Not only did she always bring in something scrumptious for the break room that he could nibble on all day and night, she was something worth looking at for the next twenty-four hours.

Certainly, Cynthia would also keep his mind off the French heiress.

Curtis wasn't disappointed.

The spread Cynthia put out was enormous. It wasn't anything too special, but a crock-pot of soup, bread, and meats for sandwiches, and a great, big tray of chocolate chip cookies. Curtis was guilty. He took six and shoved them in his locker knowing they'd be gone before he came back in for a cup of soup or a sandwich.

"I have to admit," he said leaning over the counter of the nurses' station, "I was mighty glad to see you were on for the twenty-four shift."

"Were you?" She winked her crystal blue eye and slid a brilliant smile over her slightly pouty lips.

To the average eye the woman in the floral print scrubs, a blonde knot of hair on her head, and white Nike shoes wasn't much to look at. But to Dr. Keller, who had seen what lay beneath the shapeless uniform while golden locks of curls fell over her shoulders, it wasn't hard to imagine at all.

"What kind of soup?"

"Wedding."

He snarled his upper lip. "Wedding soup?"

"Uh-huh." She shuffled through the papers in front of her.

"Just a wedding week I suppose." He walked around the desk and sat down on the counter next to where she sat in the chair.

Cynthia looked up at him. "Your brother?"

"Yep. Third marriage. Second marriage in two months. Second marriage to first wife." He fingered the tiny hoop that hung from her ear. "Sounds like a soap opera, doesn't it?"

"We all love a soap opera."

"I suppose we do." The pager on his waist beeped and he looked at it quickly. "Looks like my first ten year-old of the evening has a broken arm. I'll catch you around."

"I'm sure you will."

He hopped off the counter and walked back around the desk before taking a step back.

"Hey, you up for a family dinner on Sunday?"

She leaned back in her chair. "You haven't taken me to one of those in a long time."

"Because you were flirting with my brother-in-law's employee." He raised his eyebrows playfully.

"Oh, yeah. Handsome older gentleman." She laughed easily and it shot right through him. "Sure. I'd love to come."

"Great. Carlos and Madeline get back from their honeymoon Saturday. No slide shows I promise."

"Madeline, that's the ex-wife, new-wife." She punctuated the series with her finger in the air.

"Yep."

"She's the one who had cancer last year."

He nodded as his pager beeped again. "I'll fill you in. Gotta go." He ran off toward the room of the ten year-old who couldn't quite master the skill of a wheelie on his bicycle.

SIMONE SAT AT THE KITCHEN TABLE WITH REGAN AND TYLER. HE'D changed so much since she'd seen him only a few months earlier. He was ten months old and his father couldn't stop bragging about him whenever she'd phoned. Likewise, his grandmother, Madam Audrey, talked about him insensibly as well. He was certainly a cherished little boy.

Simone's parents never doted on her the way Regan and Zach did with Tyler. It made her wonder if they had once. Back before her father began taking mistresses and her mother spent her life trying to take her father's money. As far back as she could remember it had been nannies and boarding schools for her. They had conveniently locked her away and forgotten about her — mostly.

BERNADETTE MARIE

It was old news now, she decided. She was a grown woman in her mid-thirties and her fate was now her own. Besides, she couldn't get to her mother and her father's money was no longer within her reach. The secure life of Simone Pierpont was over. But she told herself that too was normal. Not everyone had millions of dollars at their disposal, or drivers, or homes in multiple countries. No, what she had always deemed as the usual was in fact not. If she expected any empathy toward her situation she needed to tread lightly. If anyone really knew what she came from they'd turn her away as quickly as they would a homeless person begging for food and shelter at their suburban front door.

She watched as Regan, very discreetly, unbuttoned her shirt and Tyler latched on to her breast. Even within the confines of her own home, not much was shown that would embarrass any guest.

Zach walked into the kitchen in white shorts and a matching Polo shirt. He poured himself a cup of coffee. "Ah, two of my favorite women sharing coffee at the table. Beautiful way to start my morning."

Regan shifted her head to look up at her husband. "Where are you off to so cheerfully?"

"Mom scheduled us a doubles match at her club. I think she's showing me off."

"At least she's not doing it to try and marry you off anymore." Regan flashed him a smile.

Simone remembered Audrey always trying to find the perfect wife for her son, before Regan had happened into his life. Then he'd never had eyes for anyone else.

Zach sipped his coffee. "I think she's trying to marry herself off."

"Hmm, well then pick her a good one." Regan laughed as she caught Tyler's hand and let his fingers wrap around her finger.

Simone tucked her lips between her teeth to keep them from quivering at the sight. It was a precious sight.

18

She watched Tyler's little head bob as he suckled his mother and his hand caressed her exposed skin. A lump caught in her throat and she swallowed it back.

Zach set his coffee mug on the table and bent down to kiss his son. His lips lingered on his forehead as Tyler continued to nurse. Then Zach lifted his head, gazed into his wife's eyes and smiled before pressing a kiss on her lips.

"I'll be back in a few hours. Can I get you anything?"

Regan's cheeks flushed and she tried to fight the smile that Simone watched creep across her lips. "I'm craving a chocolate candy bar."

"I don't know why I asked." He kissed her again. "Goodbye my lovely, Simone. *Ayez un beau jour.*"

"*Oui,*" she said knowing it was always a nice day in his home and with his wife. "Give Madam Audrey my best, will you."

"I will." He kissed her on the cheek, picked up his coffee, and headed out the door.

Simone sat and watched as Regan skillfully turned Tyler around on her lap and he latched on to the other breast. She picked up her mug, hoping it didn't seem as if she were staring. "Does that hurt?"

"Nursing? No. It's an amazing experience." Regan let out a breath. "But this will be the last week I nurse this big guy. As of Saturday we will begin to wean him."

"Why?"

There was a slight smile that turned up the corners of Regan's mouth, but Simone watched as she carefully controlled it.

"He's getting big. He'll be walking in a few months and it's just time."

Simone nodded. Would she enjoy nursing her child, she couldn't help but wonder watching Regan look down at her son with such love in her eyes. One thing was for sure, money or no money, she wasn't going to shuffle her child off as her parents had done to her. She'd find a way to give her baby everything he or she would ever need, but mostly, she would give her baby love.

ONCE CURTIS FREED HIMSELF FROM THE HOSPITAL, HE SPENT THE next day sleeping. His regular shift of thirty-six hours, added with being called in a day early, and then an accident on the highway, which kept him plenty busy for almost another day, he figured he was due.

It was hard to imagine having a job that didn't keep you locked up for almost a week at a time. The better part was that he loved it.

On Sunday afternoon he headed to Cynthia's to pick her up for dinner. He'd promised her he'd swing by a little early and look at a leaky faucet she had before they headed to his parents' house. A plumber she was not, but he figured she was doing him a favor having dinner with him and his family. It was the least he could do so he'd do his best to fix the leak. He hadn't told her she was supposed to be a distraction, hoping that no one would bring up the fact that Simone had showed up to the wedding.

When Cynthia swung open the front door, Curtis felt every muscle in his body, especially the ones in his jeans, stiffen. She was stunning. Her hair fell over her shoulders in loose, blonde curls, and how he was going to wiggle her out of those tight jeans he wasn't sure, but he knew by the end of the night she'd let him try.

Cynthia stepped forward, gripped his shoulders, and planted a big, wet kiss on his lips.

Curtis smiled as she pulled away. "Well the last time you ate at my parents' house it must have made a big impression on you." He rested his hands on her hips to steady them both.

"Let's just say after the week I heard you had, I figured you needed a little…" she lifted her shoulders and let them fall, "head start on your after dinner festivities."

Heat rose in his belly. Friends with benefits were wonderful. Even better, Cynthia knew that's all they were.

"C'mon." She grabbed hold of his hand yanked him through the door. "Come look at this faucet."

She pulled him into the kitchen. The contents from under the sink sat on the counter lined in rows. The doors exposing the underside of the sink were open and she had a flashlight ready for him.

Curtis knelt down and tucked his head under the counter. He turned on the flash light and gave all the pipes a look over. "When does it leak?"

"When I turn it on." Which was what she proceeded to do and Curtis yelped, hitting his head on the drainpipe as he tried to hurry out of the confined space.

"I'm sorry." She was stumbling over him trying to turn off the water. "I didn't think. Oh, Curtis..." She stood laughing as he surfaced, face, hair, and shirt soaked. She covered her mouth. "Oh, I'm so sorry."

"Funny?"

She shook her head, but the laughter still rolled. "No. Nope, not at all," she said but the next round of laughter broke free.

Curtis shook his head and leaned over the sink shaking the water from his hair. "You know what would really be funny?"

"What?"

"Seeing what you'd look like all wet." With that, he turned on the faucet, grabbed hold of the spray nozzle, and shot it in her direction.

Cynthia screamed and batted at the water while Curtis laughed.

When he turned off the water, she stood before him, her blouse clinging to the curves of her breasts, making the moment extremely seductive.

"Damn it, Curtis. Now I'm twice as wet as you." She held her arms out as water dripped in the floor.

"Oh, but paybacks are a bitch, honey."

She blew a wet, curl from her face. "Fix the damn sink and mop up the mess. I have to change."

"Are you sure? I'm liking that white shirt you've got on."

"You're a pig. Give me your shirt and I'll throw it in the dryer."

Curtis pulled off the designer T-shirt and tossed it at her. They were too good of friends for her to have made a move on him half-naked. She only shook her head and stormed off. He mopped up the floor with kitchen towels from the drawer and then got busy tightening the pipe he could see had come lose.

CHAPTER 5

*C*urtis brought his mother flowers, his father a six-pack of Bud Light, and because Cynthia told him he had to, he also bought two bottles of champagne to toast the bride and groom. He thought they should pop for the champagne since they'd made him get dressed up twice in two months in some over used monkey suit, but he did as she said.

He pushed open the front door of his childhood home. The scents from the kitchen were enticing and the sound of some sporting event poured from the family room. It was hard not to kick off your shoes and run through the house, Curtis thought.

His mother came from the kitchen wiping her hands on her apron. A huge smile crossed apricot painted lips.

"Cynthia," she called out, her German accent mixing with her Southern one. She leaned in and kissed both her cheeks. "It's so nice to have you in our home again."

"Thank you, Mrs. Keller." Cynthia handed his mother the flowers and she buried her face in them.

"Thank you."

"They're from Curtis, but his hands are full." He slanted a look at her but accepted the kindness that she'd made him sound heroic.

Curtis handed his mother one of the bottles of champagne he carried. "I brought bubbly to celebrate the newlyweds. Or is it old-weds?"

Cynthia took the other bottle from him then pushed past him and with an arm around his mother's shoulders. He heard her ask what was for dinner as they disappeared into the kitchen. Curtis headed toward his father in the family room to share the beer he had brought.

The door opened again and Carlos and his family flooded into the house. That was a wonderful sight. The kids kicked off their shoes. The boys piled onto the couch to watch the game on the TV while Clara headed straight for the kitchen already calling to her grandmother. Curtis watched as Carlos kissed his wife in the hallway and lingered a thoughtful look at her. Today she wore a hat he'd seen once before. As a doctor he knew women sometimes took a while to become comfortable with the thin hair that grew back after cancer. Madeline was no different. She caught his eye and gave him a smile before turning toward the kitchen.

Carlos stepped into the family room and slapped Curtis on the shoulder. "What's the score?"

"Dunno. Wasn't paying attention." Curtis looked back at the TV.

Eduardo looked up. "Six. Two." He looked back down at the phone in his hand as it vibrated.

"Who you texting?" Curtis inched over the arm of his chair to look, but Eduardo pulled back the phone.

"He has a new girlfriend." Carlos' other son, Christian scoffed trying to see the game.

"Girlfriend?" Curtis exchanged glances with Carlos and then looked back toward Eduardo. "You're much too young for a girlfriend."

"Oh, that's not the impressive part," Carlos sat down on the arm of the couch. "She's a senior. He took her to prom."

"That's right." He did remember hearing about that. "Uncle Zach gave you a job to pay for it."

Eduardo shoved the phone in his back pocket. "Is my life everyone's business?" He looked up at Carlos.

"In this family it is. No one is spared." Carlos winked at his him. "Take Uncle Curtis. He brought his safe date."

Curtis dropped his shoulders and stared at his brother. "My safe date? What the hell does that mean?"

"Cynthia. She in the kitchen, right?"

"So?"

"So that hot French chick is staying with our sister and you bring the safe date."

Curtis could feel the heat in his cheeks as he watched the amusement danced in his brother's eyes. "I have nothing to do with the French chick."

Carlos laughed as he stood. "No, I think she didn't have anything to do with you."

He slapped him on the shoulder again and Curtis tensed as his brother walked toward the kitchen. Fifteen years ago he would have kicked his ass for such a comment. But Curtis was mature enough to know beating up someone's father, right in front of them, wasn't mature.

So this was what they all thought? That the French chick didn't want to have anything to do with him? He sulked back into his seat, why wouldn't they think that? His own brother-in-law had to send for him when she'd stranded him on the stupid yacht.

Curtis balled his fists. Safe date. He let out a grunt which had Eduardo's head shooting up. He gave the kid a nod and stood from his seat. He wasn't going to let Simone Pierpont get under his skin. So what if she was still in town and staying with Zach and Regan. She wasn't there because he'd been thinking of her excessively for the past two months. Nope, he couldn't care less.

25

He opened his hands and wiped his sweaty palms on his pant legs as he walked toward the kitchen. As he passed through the hallway the front door opened again. This time it was Regan, who walked through with Tyler on her hip. The very sight brought a smile to Curtis' lips. He walked straight to her and reached for the toddler who stretched his arms out toward him.

"You look tired," he said kissing his sister on the cheek.

"I've been sick all week."

He bounced Tyler on his hip. "Morning sickness?"

"Why do they call it that?" She asked in a whisper, as to not let her secret out, he knew. "I'm sick all the damn time. Not just the morning."

"It'll get better."

Regan shook her head. "You talk like a doctor. You should have to feel this before you try to use your bedside manner."

He laughed, gave Tyler a squeeze with his arm, and looked back at the front door as Zach pulled open the screen. He gave Curtis a nod then stepped back as he let Simone step through.

CHAPTER 6

*T*he look on his face said it all. Simone was the last person he'd expected, or wanted, to see. She stepped into the house and swallowed the lump that had lodged in her throat. Awkward situations were something she was trained to overcome. As an heiress she was often expected to enter a room, smile, and own it. She saw no reason that this should be any different.

Simone lifted her chin, locked her eyes on Curtis, and curved her lips into the seductive smile she'd used on him months earlier.

"Hello, Curtis."

His jaw tightened and he shifted his nephew against his shoulder. "Simone. You look nice."

She kept her eyes on him. This was something she'd been trained to do. If she could pique his interest long enough, she'd have power over the conversation and Curtis would be compelled to need her, and that was just what she wanted from him.

The silence in the hallway had become strained and awkward. Zach pushed his way between them and took his son from his brother-in-law. "C'mon, big man, let's see what grandma has for you."

Regan followed her husband leaving Simone alone with the man she'd come back to America for. The very man, who now looked at her and made her want to run in the other direction. Things were not as they were when she'd left him that sunny morning. No, he hated her now.

Curtis crossed his arms over his chest. "I didn't know you'd be coming tonight." His voice dripped with disdain for her.

She gave a slight tilt to her head, which she knew showed off her best side. "Zach thought it would be rude to leave me at home."

"Great." Curtis turned to walk away.

"Curtis." She let his name float on the seductive air of her voice. He stopped and turned back to her. "I want to be friends."

"Sure. As long as you're visiting we can be friends," he said through gritted teeth.

Simone pursed her lips. "I am not visiting. I will be living here now."

He stepped closer to her, his eyes narrowed defensively. "Living here? As in living with Zach? Here in Nashville?"

She dropped her shoulders. "Yes. In my own place, but yes, that is what I mean."

He gave a slow, deep nod. "I'm sure that makes him very happy to know you'll be nearby. I'll bet Benson, Benson, and Hart has a cushy penthouse apartment in some new building that will suite you just fine."

She watched him walk away from her. Curtis didn't care that she'd come back to America for good. He thought she was just some spoiled brat, which she couldn't argue with.

Clenching her fists into balls until her nails dug into her palms, Simone fought back tears that threatened to weaken her facade. Nothing was going the way she'd hoped.

Simone followed the sounds of the family to the kitchen.

Emily and Clara chopped vegetables at the counter. Madeline stirred the sauce in the pot on the stove. Regan nursed Tyler at the table and shared a laugh with a strikingly beautiful blonde.

Regan noticed her standing in the doorway. "Simone, this is Cynthia." She nodded toward the woman next to her.

Cynthia stood and Simone knew protocol. She walked toward her, head high, shoulders back, fake smile pressed on her lips. "Cynthia, it is a pleasure to meet you."

"Oh, you're the French gal," she said with enthusiasm and wide eyes the moment she'd heard Simone's voice. "Curtis told me 'bout you."

She was surprised the woman was smiling. Curtis couldn't have shared anything good about her. She'd seen the look in his eyes when she walked in the door.

Cynthia was obviously native to Nashville. Perhaps she was a neighbor he'd grown up with. Someone who might have been at Carlos' wedding, she hoped.

Carlos and Curtis both walked through the door to the kitchen, each with a beer in their hand.

Carlos stepped in behind his wife and wrapped his arms around her waist. He placed a kiss on her neck and Simone watched her lean back against him.

"Whose winning the game?" Madeline asked on a sigh.

"Dunno. Don't care." He kissed her again.

Curtis didn't say a word as he walked past Simone and stood behind Cynthia. He placed his hand on her waist and just as Carlos had done to his wife, and lingered kiss on her neck, just above her collar bone. Cynthia laughed and shrugged him off, but a sharp pain hit Simone in the chest. She knew what that felt like to have his lips pressed to her skin.

Curtis pulled from his beer and nodded in Simone's direction. "You two met?"

Cynthia elbowed him in the gut. "Yes. At least your sister has some manners."

Regan propped Tyler up on her shoulder and patted his back. "Simone, come sit with us."

At that very moment she wasn't sure she could. Her legs had stiffened and her stomach churned. She'd be damned if she'd show weakness in front of him, even if she did want to run to the bathroom and throw up the very little bit that she'd been able to eat at lunch.

With the grace she'd been trained to have, she took a seat next to Regan.

Tyler had quickly fallen asleep on his mother's shoulder and Regan rubbed his back. "Simone, will you hold him? I need to fix my shirt."

There was no time to say no. Regan lifted him from her shoulder and handed the sleeping baby to Simone. The only option was to place him against her shoulder, just as Regan had done.

CURTIS KNEW CYNTHIA HAD FELT HIM TENSE BESIDE HER, BUT SHE didn't call him on it. Not yet. But he couldn't help the feeling that had washed over him when Simone cradled Tyler to her shoulder. It was completely unnatural, but at the same time, there was a peace to her he'd never seen. He wasn't even sure she knew she'd kissed the top of his head and closed her eyes.

Clara dropped a spoon as she carried silverware to the table and that seemed to snap him from his lock on Simone, but not before she raised her eyes and caught his stare.

Damn. What had that woman done to his heart?

Regan stood from her seat. "Oh, Clara, let me help you. If this family gets any bigger we'll have to rent a banquet hall."

Emily shook a finger in the air. "I have four grandkids and four children. I should have many more grandkids than I already do."

Curtis felt the heat on his back begin to rise. "I'm going to step outside and get some air." He looked down at Cynthia. "C'mon."

The look she shot back at him said he'd be due for a fight later, but she followed him out the back door.

As soon as the door was closed she crossed her arms in front of her and stared at him. "You're sure bossy tonight. That little French things got you all giddy."

"That little French thing? God, you're as bad as everyone else." He raked his fingers through his hair.

"What was with your reaction to her holding the baby? I'd think you're getting sentimental on me, Keller."

He didn't like her tone. He didn't like his reaction. There was always one way to fight a fire, with another fire.

Curtis turned and gathered Cynthia in his arms and pressed his mouth to hers. When she'd found her balance she wrapped her arms around him and accepted his heated kiss. He took it deeper, pushing her up against the railing of the porch.

With his teeth he nipped at her bottom lip. His hands dug into her shirt pulling her closer to him.

Finally, she put her hand on his chest and pushed back until their lips parted.

Cynthia sucked in a deep breath. "Damn. She has you more riled up than I thought."

Curtis took a step back and shoved his hands into the front pockets of his jeans. "What does that mean? I'm kissing you, not her."

"Right." Cynthia nodded, but her lips turned up in a grin. "Don't think I didn't have plans to keep you all night, but, honey, I'm not where your heart is."

"She dumped me on a yacht in the middle of the damn ocean."

This time she laughed. "And how many men can say that?"

"How many men want to?"

"Get over it. Something happened to make her leave you in the middle of nowhere. She's here. Get to the bottom of it."

Perhaps that was the most sense he'd heard out of anyone since the incident happened.

He nodded. "I'll do that."

"Good. Now can we go back inside and help with dinner? Unless you wanted to roll behind those bushes by the garage."

Now she was sassing him and it felt normal.

"Maybe later. Mom's got a pie in the oven. Pie first." He wrapped his arm around her waist and they walked back into the house.

CHAPTER 7

Simone listened to Carlos and his family share their stories of the honeymoon they had all taken. Zach had confided in her, before their wedding, that he was sending them to Disney World in style. They were a family, and they deserved to celebrate the union of their marriage as such.

She felt bad now, listening to them discuss the trip in enthusiastic detail, that she'd laughed at Zach. A honeymoon was to be spent on a beach, or on a yacht. She'd thought she'd always wanted to go to Fiji and spend her honeymoon naked in a hut with her husband. But she could see again, her upbringing was getting in the way of what the rest of the world thought was perfect. For the Kellers, Disney World was the perfect oasis to spend their second honeymoon as a family.

Carlos and Madeline held hands atop the table among the many dishes that were passed around with ample amounts of food on them. Simone watched as their eyes settled on each other, and their lips were permanently turned into smiles. She wondered if anyone would know what they'd been through, and that they'd been in love since they'd been fifteen.

Divorce, second marriages, and cancer hadn't kept them apart in the end. What was it like to love someone so much?

She turned and looked at Zach and Regan who balanced a toddler between them as they reached for food and added to the conversation happening around them. There was a peace — a comfort—between them that Simone had never seen in her home growing up. They worked together as the executive team that they were. But love radiated between them.

Emily Keller sat at one end of the crowded table and her husband Alan sat at the other. They didn't look at each other. They passed plates and talked to their children and grandchildren, and yet, love resonated in their voices. Simone knew nothing about them, really, except that they'd brought together this eclectic family with love and compassion. And the fact that they would all gather together once a week for dinner said something about their marriage. You didn't have a family like the Keller family without understanding true love.

The food on Simone's plate began to look unappetizing. Not because it was ill prepared or unpalatable, but because she realized how out of place she was at the family table. Her parents despised each other long before they divorced and married others. Simone's family had been the children at school, and of course the awkward American boy who had been thrown into the a mix of friends at an early age. Zach and his parents had shown her a compassion she'd never known, and yet it was nothing like the Kellers.

Zach passed her a plate of mashed potatoes and gave her a comforting smile. "Everything okay?"

"A bit overwhelmed."

"I'm glad you're here. It's a very important night."

He turned back to his wife, but his words stuck with her. Had she missed something? Was there something more than Sunday dinner or the fact that Madeline and Carlos had returned? She lifted her head and looked at Curtis and Cynthia who shared a laugh between them.

Simone felt a bead of sweat roll down the back of her neck. The room had grown hot. What if the important night had something to do with Curtis and Cynthia? Could she keep her emotions in tact when they announced they were going to get married? Obviously he'd moved on from her. Perhaps she'd been a fling to him, and not the other way around as she'd convinced herself. What was she going to do now?

A moment later Zach stood up from the table. He looked down at his wife and then out at the others at the table who had grown quiet.

He pulled Regan to his side and took Tyler from her, balancing him on his hip. "Regan and I have been waiting to share some news with all of you." He wrapped his arm around her and she rested her head against his shoulder. "We are expecting another baby."

The moment his announcement had been made, the rest of the family at the table stood and rushed the small family to Simone's side. They hugged and kissed them. Madeline and Emily cried. Carlos slapped Zach on the shoulder. Even Cynthia embraced them both and planted a noisy kiss on Tyler's cheek.

But Simone sat quiet, afraid of what she'd say.

Zach sat back down and the platters of food began to move around the table again. He touched her arm. "Are you okay? Aren't you happy for us?"

"Oh, I am very happy for you." She forced the smile that was deserved by a friend. "Congratulations."

"Can you imagine how beautiful my daughter would be if she looked just like her mother?" And it was words like that which had always set her heart a flutter when it came to Zach, but now she sat next to him feeling the sting of jealousy as if she were a sister.

He shifted a gaze to his wife and Simone thought she might

burst into tears. Would a man ever look at her like that? Would Curtis ever look at her like that or would he hate her forever?

It wasn't that she wasn't happy for them. No one deserved such a happy moment more than Zach and his wife. But her own predicament had her heart filled with bitterness, her stomach churning with fear, and a cloud of loneliness enveloping her.

CURTIS SLAMMED THE FRONT DOOR OF CYNTHIA'S HOUSE WHEN they arrived after dinner at his parents' house. She turned and glared at him with anger brewing in her eyes.

"Was that necessary?"

"Sorry, guess I have a little adrenaline running through me." Curtis ran his hands over his head and rested them on the back of his neck. He could feel the tension in his shoulders and it ran across his chest. "Too bad the gym isn't open."

Cynthia tossed her purse on the couch. "I'd offer to take care of that for you, but since I know it's a woman who has you so worked up. I think I'll save my offer for another day."

Curtis dropped his arms and she crossed hers in front of her.

"Did you think I didn't notice how worked up you got over Simone? Oh, she's got you all tied up in knots."

"Well she worked me over."

Cynthia dropped her arms and her eyes softened. "She got into your heart."

"Bite your tongue." The woman was delusional. What was wrong with the women in his life?

She laughed and shook her head as she moved toward the kitchen. "Men are dumb."

There were still towels lining the floor where they had sprayed each other and to catch any leaks from the dripping faucet. She gathered them up and headed to the laundry room.

Curtis followed her and when she dumped the towels into the washer she turned back around and ran right into him.

"What's with you?" She nudged him out of the way. This time she headed for the refrigerator and pulled out a bottle of water. She held it out to him and he waved it off. "So are you staying or what?"

"I didn't think there was much of an invitation."

"There is always an invitation. But I think tonight it's just a *sleep* over. Your head is in the clouds and your mind is wrapped around that little French lady."

"French, maybe. Lady? That's a stretch." He jammed his hands into his pockets and leaned back against the counter. "Did you see how she reacted to Zach when he announced the baby?"

"So. It's no secret she's always liked Zach. Even I know that and I've only been around him a few times."

"She liked him when they were kids, Cynthia." He took the bottle of water out of her hands and drank from it before handing it back to her. "She's not in love with him."

"I don't think she acted as if she wasn't happy."

"No, but she should have been the first one out of her seat to hug him and congratulate them."

Cynthia sipped from the bottle. "I told you she got you all worked up." She finished the water and threw the bottle into the recycle bin. "You watched her all night long. I'll bet you even know what she left on her plate."

He winced. Of course he did, she hadn't touched a thing. In fact, he didn't think she looked well at all. It was probably nerves. After all, having dinner with the Keller family for the first time was probably nerve wracking, no matter what your relationship was with the people at the table.

Cynthia moved in closer to him and placed her hand on his chest. She looked up at him and batted her lashes. "I'm going to bed. Why don't you go home and get some sleep. I'm off tomorrow. You?" He nodded. "Good. You're going to meet me at noon for lunch. And we're going to sort out what's going on in that head of yours."

"I don't think that sounds like fun at all."

"Curtis Keller, I've spent more time with you than any other woman has in the past three years. You're one of my dearest friends." She tapped her fingers against his chest. "That woman has wrapped herself so tightly around your heart you're going to explode. We'd better figure out what you're going to do about it."

"I don't want to do anything about it. She doesn't deserve it."

She wrapped her arms around his neck and settled a friendly look on him. "Don't you suppose there's a reason she came back to Nashville?"

Again, he winced. Yeah, she wasn't the kind to just decide to move somewhere without an ocean to escape on. Something was up and he figured he'd better find out what. After all, if Simone Pierpont was up to something, it could seriously affect his sister and her family. He couldn't let that happen.

CHAPTER 8

Simone paced the floor in her bedroom. She'd been embarrassed by her reaction when Zach announced that they were expecting another baby. Of all people she should have jumped up from her chair and kissed his cheek and squeezed his wife. That was protocol for something like that. Instead she'd sat there.

She dropped into the oversized chair by the window and let her head fall back. Maybe no one else had noticed her reaction. Oh, that was just foolish to think that way. Curtis had noticed.

Well things were certainly different now. She couldn't stay with Zach and Regan any longer. Certainly she couldn't tell them about her predicament now that they were ecstatic to have their own baby. Her father had pushed her away. She'd dishonored him—embarrassed him. There was no crawling back to him, and her mother—well she wasn't even sure where her mother was at the moment.

First things first, she needed to get a job, find a place to live, and then, and only then, could she tell Curtis about the baby. She needed to prove, to herself and to him—and the rest of the world—that she could handle this responsibility. Indeed she was old enough. Somewhere in her private schooling and her etiquettes classes she had to have been taught how to take on the world without a butler and a chauffeur.

When her father saw his grandchild he'd want to accept her back. Her world would return to normal. Curtis would want her too. He wasn't the kind to turn away family.

Thoughts of his parents and his brothers and their wives clouded her mind. Curtis Keller might never turn her and their baby away, but would he ever love her as the other men loved their wives?

Tears stung her eyes and she let them fall. She hated the thoughts she was having. Her baby wasn't some tool to get a man, or regain her wealth. Hadn't that been what her mother had done?

No. She'd make a life for herself first. If it was just her and the baby, so be it. Women did it all the time. She could do it too.

The tears began to dry up and there was a sense of pride swelling in her chest. Simone Pierpont was somebody, not just some heiress with a yacht and a stunning wardrobe. She'd prove that she could make it on her own and provide for another.

Simone sucked in a breath and embraced the new sense of self-worth, which felt better than the acquisition of a new diamond bracelet or a custom made pair of Italian shoes. This was a feeling no one could pay for.

Her moment was interrupted by a tapping at the door.

"Come in," she called as she stood from the chair and wiped at her eyes quickly hoping to hide the tears she'd shed.

Regan opened the door slowly. "Am I bothering you?"

"Of course not. Please, come in."

Regan moved around the door. In her hand she carried a mug. "I made you some tea. I thought you could use it to relax."

"I appreciate it. Thank you." She took the mug from Regan and sat back down in the chair.

"Simone, I hope I'm not overstepping my boundaries, but is everything alright with you?

"I beg your pardon."

Regan sat down on the bed across the room and laid her hands in her lap. "Zach is worried about you. He says you're not yourself."

"He worries too much, that is all."

"Perhaps. But you mean a great deal to him, and to me too. If there is anything wrong, we want to help."

Simone thought of all the things she could tell Regan. She'd always wanted a sister, and Regan was as close as she'd come. But still, there was no way to tell her what had transpired in her life, after all, Regan was Curtis' sister. Telling her what she'd done could change her relationship with the woman forever. She'd already been thrown out of her father's life, she couldn't risk Zach and his wife throwing her out too.

"Everything is fine. I have just been having a moment of clarity, before you walked in." She tucked her feet under her and smiled at Regan. "I've decided I want to find my own place to live and get a job."

The reaction on Regan's face should have made her angry, but she knew it was genuine. When an oil heiress tells you she wants to get a job most people would stare at her wide eyed with their mouths open, just as Regan was doing.

"I think that's great. So you'll be staying in Nashville longer than you'd anticipated?"

"I want to. I think it is time."

"Simone, I think that's wonderful." And from the compassion in Regan's eyes she knew she was sincere. "Zach could surely…"

Simone held up her hand to stop her. "I will not take a job or a home from him."

"But, Simone…"

"No. I will do this myself. I can do this."

Regan stood and walked toward her. She bent down and gave

41

her a warm hug. "I know you can. I believe you are the kind of woman who gets what she wants."

Simone bit the inside of her cheek. She could only hope that was in fact the kind of woman she was.

Regan took a step back. "I'll let you get some sleep. Perhaps we could go to lunch tomorrow and discuss your plans. I'm a great assistant and I'm dying to do something. Maybe I can help you work on your resume, or hunt down some places to live."

"I think that sounds splendid."

"Great. Good night."

"Good night." Regan turned to leave and Simone stood quickly. "Oh, and, Regan," she waited for her to turn. "Congratulations on the new baby. I know Zach wants a house full of children."

"I hope so. Coming from a big family I want Tyler to have that."

Regan shut the door and Simone was alone again, but this time she didn't feel alone. No, she had someone to take care of and she and Regan were going to make plans for her new life. She sucked in a deep breath and let it out slowly. Was she ready for a new life? She placed her hands on her stomach. Well, ready or not, it was coming.

CHAPTER 9

Curtis pulled the lettuce off his sandwich, reassembled the bread, and then pushed it aside. Cynthia sipped her Pepsi and shook her head. "You're not going to eat?"

"Just not hungry."

Cynthia picked up her sandwich and took a bite. "Have you met Sam yet?"

"Sam?"

"Male nurse. Six-four. Short blond hair. Dreamy blue eyes."

Curtis let out a loud chuckle. "No, guess I've missed him."

"He's working at the clinic with me on my days off at the hospital. And he's taking me out to dinner tonight."

Curtis pulled his sandwich back toward him and took a bite. He was more comfortable now that they were talking about her rather than the conversation they'd been having about him and Simone. "Do I need to shake him down and make sure he's worthy of taking you out?"

"You even talk to him I'll shove you in your locker."

And that was why he adored his friendship with Cynthia. He could take her to a ball game, or a fancy dinner. If they felt like it, they'd tangle up the sheets. Or she could abuse him and tell him all about her sex life with other men. He realized he was lucky. Every man should have that very special woman in their lives. The ones who would do anything for you or with you, but didn't come with strings attached.

"Oh, my gosh. Your sister is here." Cynthia's hand went up in a wave and Curtis turned his head to the door. "Oh, look. She's with Simone."

He felt the bread from his sandwich lodge in his throat. He reached for his drink and the women approached the table.

"Fancy meeting you here." Regan reached past Curtis and gave Cynthia a casual hug and then gave him a quick peck on the cheek. "Simone and I were just grabbing some lunch."

"Oh, sit with us," Cynthia was quick to add.

Suddenly Curtis' appetite was completely gone. His sister pulled out a chair and Simone took the vacant one next to him. He lifted his eyes to see her, but she'd kept hers diverted. All the better he thought.

"Simone, how are you? Is this heat enough for you? At least you've come when it will start to cool off." Cynthia asked a little too enthusiastically for him.

"It has been pleasant."

Curtis picked up his drink again. Maybe he could just drown in the cup. But then the next best thing happened. The pager on his hip went off and he reached for it as quickly as he could. "Ah, they need me at the hospital."

"I didn't know you were on call." Cynthia looked at him as he stood from the table.

"They called this morning and said Drake was out sick. I'll catch you ladies later." He picked up his sandwich and made sure he kissed Cynthia goodbye before he darted out the door. Thank goodness for someone's tragedy.

. . .

SIMONE COULDN'T DECIDE IF SHE WAS GLAD THAT CURTIS HAD LEFT or if she'd rather have him near and just remain awkward in his presence. There was a comfort in that too.

The waitress stopped at the table, left glasses of water, and took their orders. The moment she walked away Simone reached for the water and began to drink it down. If only it were champagne and it would wash away any self-doubt she had sitting across from Curtis' girlfriend.

Cynthia reached over to the plate Curtis had taken his sandwich from, and ate a chip. As she bit into it Simone thought of how intimate and unassuming it was, and Curtis wasn't even there. She sipped her water again and hoped Cynthia didn't realize how uncomfortable she was. A Pierpont was never to appear shaken or uncomfortable.

Cynthia took another chip. "So, Regan, how are you feeling?"

"I feel better every day, but I look forward to the end of this first trimester."

Cynthia gave her a nod then turned toward Simone. "And are you getting situated? Curtis said you were planning on staying in Nashville for a while."

Simone swallowed hard. She was trained to have etiquette when spoken to. A Pierpont had poise. There was no reason that she couldn't carry on a conversation with the woman and be as prestigious as she'd been raised. Just because her father had taken her every last dime, and she was in some diner in Nashville instead of a posh hotel restaurant, there was no reason she shouldn't have her shoulders back and her spine straight, even if she was talking to the woman Curtis was sleeping with.

She formed her lips into a gracious smile. "I have decided to stay permanently."

Regan nudged Cynthia as she'd seen casual friends do. "That's what we're doing today. I'm her executive assistant today. We're seeking out jobs and places to live."

"Now that sounds like fun." Cynthia took another chip and

then sat up straight. "Are you looking for anything specific in a job?"

"Oh, not really. I have never had a job outside of my father's company. I look forward to something new." She hoped she conveyed that so that the desperateness of the situation didn't come through. It wasn't that she looked forward to something new; she was now desperate for it.

"You can type can't you?"

"Yes. I am quite proficient in it."

Cynthia's eyes grew wide. "They have an opening at the clinic."

"Clinic?"

"Yeah, I work at a medical clinic on the weekends. But they have a full time position for clerical."

Regan patted her arm. "Oh, that would be great."

The noise from the small diner was closing in on her. Was the woman Curtis made sure he kissed in front of her actually offering to help her find a job? Was she desperate enough to accept her help? "I do not know anything about medical."

Cynthia leaned back in her seat and laughed. "Well it's not like they're asking you to do surgery. It's all data entry. Put the information in the computer and file the paperwork. I'm telling you, if you're willing to work I can get you in."

Simone looked to Regan for support, but she was only grinning wide.

Cynthia sat back up in her seat and gave Simone a serious look. "Wait, if you need a job why don't you just ask Zach. I thought you were best friends or something."

"Zachary is my very dearest friend. But no, I am not asking him for a job. I want to do this all on my own."

Cynthia gave her a slow nod. "Ah, so this is one of those *I'm showing the world I can make it on my own* gigs?" She took another chip from Curtis' plate. "I mean, we all need to stand up for ourselves at some point, right?"

"Right."

"My dad owns a garden shop. You know, fertilizer, plants, the whole garden gamut. But I didn't like bugs and dirt." She laughed as she lifted her drink to her lips and took a sip. "He was furious when I told him I didn't want to do flowers the rest of my life. He was even madder when I told him I wanted to be a nurse."

"A nurse is a very noble career." Simone couldn't imagine someone scoffing at such a job choice.

"Yeah, but his feelings were hurt. He'd built this business with the thought the kids would take it over and I had other plans. He got over it, but I remember wanting to get a job, on my own, and move out, on my own. So I worked at McDonald's for minimum wage during the day and went to school for nursing on the weekends. I lived in a tiny apartment just off campus and ate noodles every day of my life for years." Her eyes sparkled. "It was the hardest thing I ever did, but I did it."

Simone never thought she'd bond with the other woman in Curtis' life. In fact, she wanted desperately to hate her. But they did understand each other. Perhaps Cynthia hadn't escaped an oil empire, but she obviously knew what it meant to show the world she could make it on her own. Her enthusiasm was contagious and it was exactly what Simone knew she needed to make it through.

"Do you think they would hire me?"

"Of course." Cynthia batted away the comment with her hand as if she'd be the one to hire her. "Why don't we head down there and you can fill out the application."

Again Simone looked to Regan for her approval.

"I seem to be one great assistant." She yawned and then rubbed her still flat stomach. "I got you a job just by having lunch." Regan laughed.

"So you think this is a good idea?"

"Of course I do. And if you're going to head out with Cynthia, I'm going to head home and take a nap."

CHAPTER 10

*S*imone had been in awkward situations before, but sitting in Cynthia's car as they drove through Nashville had to rank right at the top of the list of uncomfortable moments in her life.

Oh, Cynthia had been cordial enough. She pointed out restaurants she liked, talked about a man named Sam who worked at the clinic, and who Simone would probably find him nice to work with. She played with the volume on the radio three or four times and even sang along with a song Simone had never heard. However, she never seemed to act as if Simone was an obstacle in her life. Perhaps she was that comfortable with her relationship with Curtis to think that Simone wasn't a threat. Then again, maybe Curtis hated her enough that she wasn't a threat.

Cynthia pulled up to the clinic, which was within view of a hospital where Simone assumed she and Curtis both worked. That was a bit too close for comfort, but her whole motive in showing people she could make it on her own was to prove to Curtis she was worthy of him and their baby, so the location would be an asset.

Simone stepped out of the car as Cynthia skirted the front. Her blonde hair bounced in loose natural curls as if she'd only jumped out of bed and let her hair dry. She was casual in a pair of jeans and a T-shirt. But what Simone noticed most was how comfortable she was in her own skin. Simone had never had that, no matter how she carried herself.

She looked down at her own clothes. Casual, she thought, but her red high heels peeked from the bottoms of her black slacks. Her bright, billowy, flower print, silk shirt clung to her skin in the Tennessee heat. A large chunky ring adorned her right ring finger. Pearls dangled from her ears and lay against her neck and wrist. She'd left her hair down, but even she hadn't thought it looked classy enough when she'd left the house.

All put together, and she still didn't have the confidence Cynthia had as she opened the front door to the building. "Are you coming?"

"Yes. I am just a bit nervous."

"With that accent they're going to eat you up. And in a good way," she added.

All heads in the waiting area turned as they walked through the door. A few of the people gave a nod to Cynthia, but all eyes scanned over Simone. One woman seated in the corner with a baby looked up at Cynthia and she quickly moved right to her.

"Regina, what are you doing here again?" The woman looked up at her and her face had been bruised.

Simone felt her knees begin to buckle and she bent them slightly to keep from toppling over. Someone had hit the woman with the baby, and the way Cynthia looked at her, this wasn't the first time.

Regina responded to Cynthia in Spanish, but Simone didn't understand. But the message was clear.

Cynthia shook her head and then gave Regina a hug. She'd reassured her by saying something to her quietly. Regina nodded and Cynthia smiled and then ran her hand over the baby's head.

Her demeanor had changed when she headed back to Simone. "C'mon. I'll introduce you to Marsha. She's in charge."

Cynthia led her through the closed door and into the clinic. Curtains were drawn around beds. Babies were crying and chirps from machines were heard over the shuffling of feet and words spoken in whispers. Cynthia didn't seem to notice any of it as she led Simone to an office at the end of the hall.

She tapped on the open door and the large black woman who sat behind the desk smiled wide. "What are you doin' here? It's your day off."

"I brought you a new data entry clerk." She nodded to Simone.

Simone stepped into the office, which she thought might have once been a closet. There was hardly enough room for all three of them and the desk.

Marsha looked her over. "You sure look fancy for wanting to work in a clinic."

"I assure you, I can do the job, Ms..."

"Ooo, fancy French accent." Marsha shifted her glance to Cynthia. "Where did you find her?"

"Curtis Keller." His name rolled from Cynthia's tongue and it gave Simone an uneasy feeling. What would he think if he knew she was using his name to find herself a job.

"Well..." Marsha's eyes widened and lit up. She held out her hand and shook Simone's. Her large hand enveloped Simone's petite fingers. "You come with some power behind you. If you're a friend of Curtis Keller's you must be something special."

Simone would have like to have thought so, but she wasn't sure Curtis felt the same way. "Thank you. But I am quite positive that I can do the job Cynthia has proposed even without Mr. Keller's endorsement."

"Uh-huh." Marsha crossed her arms in front of her broad chest. "Well, first the name is Marsha. No need for any fancy manners here. And second, can you type?"

"Yes."

"Can you file? Fax if needed? Email?"

Simone gave her a confident smile, one she'd rehearsed most of her life. "Yes, Ms.—Marsha—I am quite proficient in all of those areas."

Marsha gave her a slow nod. "We have a dress code. You're dressed a bit too fancy for it."

Simone swallowed hard. She was quite appropriately dressed for any position in any company. "And what would the dress code be?"

"Scrubs. Can you handle that?"

"Scrubs?"

Cynthia leaned in toward her. "Like wearing your jammies to work all day."

She looked at the outfit that Marsha wore. It was purple with big pockets with sheep on it. This must be the attire they recommended, though Simone couldn't imagine why. "Oh, I am sure it won't be a problem."

Marsha nodded again, slowly. "Well, if you come with such shiny recommendations from Cynthia and Curtis you must be one hell-of-a gal."

Cynthia held up a hand as if to add more. "She comes pretty well recommended. Let me drop a few more names for you. Zach and Regan Benson and of course Audrey Benson."

"Well, girl. You are connected aren't you?"

Simone felt heat fill her cheeks. "I have been blessed with some wonderful friendships."

"Uh-huh." Marsha sat back down in her chair and pulled a file from the drawer beside her. "Here. As far as I'm concerned you're over qualified for this piddle job, but if you want it, it's yours, honey."

She handed Simone the file. "You start tomorrow at nine. Scrubs." She emphasized with a look that scanned over Simone from head to toe. "Bring in the paperwork and we'll get you started training."

Simone couldn't believe that by dropping a few names she'd landed a job. If it were this easy why were there so many people out of work? And even funnier, it wasn't her father's name that had to be dropped, but Curtis and his family's. She could do this. She could prove that she was capable of taking care of a job, and wearing scrubs—whatever they were. A hint of excitement brewed in her belly. So this was what independence felt like? She liked it.

She held out her hand to Marsha, who shook it again. "Thank you, Marsha. I appreciate the job and the opportunity."

"Girl, I think the men are going to eat up that accent." She laughed. "Oh, and you'll want to leave any of that fancy jewelry at home."

Simone looked down at her hands. Certainly that wasn't fancy jewelry she wore, but she nodded as Cynthia pushed her out of the cramped office before she turned back toward Marsha.

"Hey, Regina is back." Her voice had dropped and sadness echoed in its tone.

Marsha dropped her head and shook it. "I wish I could get that woman far from here." She sighed heavy. "I'll go out and talk to her."

Cynthia lifted her hand in a wave and they headed back through the clinic.

She showed Simone where she'd be working. It was another office, cramped much like Marsha's was, toward the back of the building. There were two desks there, but at least there was a window.

The pride that had filled Simone earlier was quickly turning into fear. The only work she'd ever really done was to look pretty for her father's investors. She was trained quite well in the art of small talk and smiling pretty. Yes, she could type well, and she knew her alphabet well enough to file, but what was she really doing? There was a fine line between successfully landing your first job and failing miserably at keeping it.

Oh, who was she kidding? This job was no different than the rest of her life. Only the name dropping had changed. But she had to admit, the names being dropped now weren't because of big money or power, it was because of influence. The names that she'd associated with to help her into her new position in life were the names of family, people who took care of others. Yes, there was in fact some pride that went with knowing the Keller family, and even more pride in knowing, no matter what the outcome, she'd be in charge of bringing another Keller into the world.

CHAPTER 11

*C*urtis had wrapped and bandaged nearly thirty people on his day off. One little boy had thrown up on him, and a baby girl had peed on him. All in all it had been a fine day, especially since he hadn't been forced to sit with Simone at lunch.

But now his stomach growled and he'd remembered only taking a few bites of his sandwich before throwing it into the trash because he'd lost his appetite. The way he saw it, Cynthia owed him a meal, especially since she was the one who made Simone sit at their table.

He'd dropped by home for a quick shower and a change of clothes before rapping on her door.

She was laughing when she opened the door with a glass of wine in her hand. Her hair was curled, and she had on his favorite pair of tight jeans. Obviously, she'd been expecting him.

"Oh, Curtis!" Her eyes widened when she said it and the laugh she'd been enjoying died down. "What are you doing here?"

"Not something you've ever asked before, doll. But I'm guessing by your expression you have company."

Cynthia bit down on her lip and stepped back to open the

door further. He stepped in just as Simone walked out of Cynthia's bedroom wearing a pair of Cynthia's scrubs.

Without looking up she walked down the hall looking over her ensemble. "Why do they think these are appealing to patients? I mean..." She looked up and her eyes locked on Curtis'. "I'm sorry. I did not hear you come in." He watched her chest rise and fall as she took in a deep, uncomfortable breath. "Hello, Curtis. How are you this evening?"

"How am I? Confused. That's how I am." He shifted his glance toward Cynthia. "What's going on?"

Her lips turned into the smile he'd seen many times before. It was the kind of smile that said she was up to something. "Simone got a new job today. She's trying on her new wardrobe."

"She what?" He spun his head back toward the French beauty in the hall. "You what?"

Cynthia shoved the glass of wine toward him. "Oh, settle down, Curtis. We got her a job at the clinic. I thought it would be fun to get some new scrubs and told her she could have a few of my others."

The thought should have caught him as funny. Simone Pierpont not only had an hourly, minimum wage job, but she was excepting hand-me-downs from someone she just met. Something was seriously wrong with the situation. But before he could protest there was another knock at the door.

Cynthia quickly moved past him and opened the door. Standing on the other side was Sam, and Curtis did in fact remember the tall, blond nurse Cynthia had mentioned she had a date with.

The moment he looked past her, his face became uncomfortable, but he smiled and gave Curtis a nod.

"Curtis, you remember Sam?" Cynthia stepped back and Sam walked into the house and extended his hand toward him.

"Nice to meet you." His deep voice resonated and his large hand enveloped Curtis' hand.

"Likewise."

Cynthia stepped between them. "And this is our friend Simone."

Curtis watched as the well trained Simone pushed back her shoulders and with a natural shift of her head, her long black hair moved over her shoulder as she smiled and slid her dainty hand toward the giant of a man.

"Sam, it is my pleasure to meet you."

"You too. French?"

"Yes. Born and raised just outside of Paris."

"Cool."

Curtis took a long sip of the wine which had been handed to him. Yeah, Cynthia had picked a winner with this one.

"Well," Cynthia looked at Curtis as she retrieved her purse from the couch. "Now that you're here, you can give Simone a ride home."

He heard Simone gasp from the hallway, but before he could look up she'd composed herself in her debutant way. How'd he walk into such a set up?

"It would be awesome if neither of you were here when I got back," Cynthia whispered as she reached for Sam's hand and walked out of the house.

As soon as the door closed he finished the wine in his hand. Simone stood watching him and that made him as angry as the situation he'd walked into.

"You got a job at the clinic?"

Simone only nodded. Cat must have gotten her tongue. That was funny. She always had something to say.

He took a step toward her, and that was when her head snapped into its defensive tilt. Oh, he was ready for a fight. Maybe it was time to let her know just how pissed he was over being left in the middle of the ocean with nothing but a swim suit.

"How is it you could land a job it one afternoon?"

"Cynthia was very gracious to vouch for me with her supervisor."

He chuckled. "You have skills an employer would want?"

Her hands came to her hips and she balled her fists. "How dare you speak to me like that."

"How dare I? Oh, I think I have every right."

She dropped her hands. "I am trying to make a new life for myself. I would think you would appreciate that."

"Oh, sure. I'd appreciate it if it were in Paris and not right under my nose."

Her mouth opened, yet she still didn't seem to have anything to say. She wasn't very good at this fighting thing, but he wasn't quite done.

"Do you have any idea what you're in for? Do you think you can show up in your pearls and your diamonds and they'll hand you a pay check? That's not how it works, doll."

Her nostrils flared and the corners of her mouth tightened. "Do not call me that."

"You're not a working stiff."

"Maybe I want to be."

"And who in their right mind would want to be?" He found he'd taken a step closer to her and she to him. Now they were standing nearly toe to toe. Her blue eyes seared through him and it wasn't a comfortable position to be in.

Curtis took a breath and let his shoulders fall. "Simone, why do you want to do this? Why move here, get a job, and wear a uniform?" He motioned to her clothing. "You don't have to do this." His voice was soft now and it irked him. Damn it he cared about her and he didn't want to.

"Did your father ever want you to do something and it was not what was in your heart?"

He thought back. He supposed there was something. But he couldn't imagine what it was. His parents had never been anything but supportive, no matter how many times they brought up the cost of educational loans.

"What is it that your father makes you do that has driven you across the world to prove him wrong?"

She looked away. He'd made her uncomfortable and he wasn't sure what to do about that. He'd wanted to pick a fight, but the nature of his job and his upbringing had him wanting to scoop her up and hold her. But he fought the urge. She deserved to be uncomfortable in his presence.

"I should get changed. If you want to leave, I will call for a taxi." She turned from him and shut the bedroom door behind her.

CHAPTER 12

*S*imone fell against the door. Was it possible for her
heart to actually explode? She placed her hand on her
chest. One moment Curtis had looked at her as if he hated her
and the next moment his eyes and voice had softened as if he still
cared. Could she possibly make the best of this horrible situation
she'd caused herself?

She changed back into her regular clothing and folded up the
scrubs Cynthia was letting her have. She'd never have imagined
she'd need to borrow uniform either, especially one with teddy
bears on it. Even worse, she couldn't afford her own uniforms
yet. This was a feeling she'd never known—utter desperation.

When she walked out of the bedroom, adjusting the pearls on
her wrist, Curtis was still there, seated on the couch.

"You are still here." She tried to keep her voice even.

"I'm not going to let you take a taxi home. It'll be dark soon
and I'm sure, no matter how many times you've been in
Nashville, you don't know your way around. And I'm darn sure
you've never called for a taxi."

He was right she had never needed a taxi, there'd always been a car waiting for her. More than likely she'd have called Zach because she couldn't afford at taxi, but she'd keep that to herself.

"I'm ready to go. Thank you in advance for the ride."

Curtis stood and scrubbed his hand over his face. The shadow of his whiskers darkened his face and gave him a rugged look. Heat stirred in her belly as he dropped his hands to his side.

"I'd showed up here looking for company for dinner. Looks like Cynthia had other plans. So what do you say? Want to grab a bite?"

It certainly was the most backward of invitations, but in her state, she thought it best to take the opportunity to be alone with him. She was going to need every second she could get to make him fall in love with her. And this time she couldn't run.

"I could use some dinner. Thank you." She reached past him for her purse on the couch and her arm brushed his. She tried not to tremble as their skin touched, but she heard him suck in his breath. Would it be wise just to look up at him and kiss him? Could she make him forget that she'd run from him—abandoned him. She swallowed hard and stood straight, but he was already backing away.

It was going to be harder than she thought to win him over again.

CURTIS WAS DRIVING AROUND IN CIRCLES, BUT HE WASN'T SURE SHE noticed. He'd thought of taking her to some diner and just getting a meal and taking her home. Then he decided she deserved something better than some greasy hamburger, so he'd started toward a nice Italian restaurant. Now he was back to thinking that if he hit McDonald's it would be good enough.

She hadn't said a word since she climbed into the passenger seat of his truck. A million questions were racing through his head. Maybe he should just drive through somewhere and park. She'd be a captive audience if he parked on some dirt road and made her tell him why she left him alone on the yacht. Didn't she think what they'd shared was important? Didn't she know how he felt about her?

And then there were the rising concerns over her moving to Nashville and taking an hourly job. Who did she really think she was trying to fit into the working class in Cynthia's hand-me-downs? She must have thought it was a great big joke to walk in there in her red high heels and pearls. He had a mind to—well he didn't know what he'd do. That was his problem. When it came to Simone Pierpont he lost all common sense.

His fingers were tensing around the steering wheel and the heat under his collar was growing almost unbearable. He turned to look at her, to sense her, to get even more worked up. She was asleep. Her head was rested against the back of the seat. Her dark hair curtained her face. God, she was beautiful.

Change of plans, he decided.

He continued down the street and headed toward home.

THE TRUCK HAD COME TO A STOP, AND SIMONE QUICKLY REALIZED her eyes were closed. She jumped up in her seat and when she looked at Curtis he was smiling at her.

"I'm sorry." She widened her eyes and tried to gather herself back up.

"Why? You must be tired." He was still smiling.

She took account of where she was and why she was with him. Certainly she couldn't be dreaming. But when she looked out the window and saw his apartment building she knew she had to be.

"I couldn't think of a thing for dinner," he said. "But I have a steak defrosted in the fridge. I could start up the grill and throw down a salad if you're up for it."

She nodded, not quite sure what he'd said, but it meant he'd brought her home and was going to spend enough time with her to feed her. She'd take that and she'd do whatever it took not to make him want to throw her out.

The apartment was just as she'd remembered it. Small. Dark. Dusty. She felt right at home knowing he was there with her.

He must have realized how dark it was. He went directly to the windows and the sliding doors that led to the patio and opened the blinds and curtains.

"Sorry. It's usually daytime when I'm sleeping. I didn't realize this place never saw the sun," he hurried around the room picking up odd pieces of clothing and dirty dishes.

"Please do not worry about it. You do not have to tidy on my account."

He gave a grunt and stopped. "You seem different."

That small statement had her hands shaking. Did he know already? She held her hands behind her back and squared off her shoulders. "I do not understand. Why do I seem different?"

He gave a shrug. "I don't know. You seem quiet, as if..." he shook his head.

"As if what?" She didn't want to raise her voice, but it teetered on the edge of annoyance. If he knew something he needed to say it. Did it seem as though she were keeping a secret?

"Nothing. I'll get dinner started. Can I get you a drink? I have some wine—I think."

Simone tried to relax. "I would love some water."

"Really, I can go get some wine."

She drew her fingers into her palms and forced sincerity into her voice. "I said water would be lovely."

He nodded slowly. "I just want you to be comfortable."

"I would be more comfortable if you would stop fussing."

He laughed. "I am fussing. I look like my mother." He set the plate in his hand on the counter. "You make me nervous."

That wasn't a positive comment. She could jump all over that, but if she did everything would go poorly the rest of the night and she'd be back to square one. "I am sorry you are uncomfortable around me. I certainly do not want that." She clasped her hands together. "Again, if you would prefer, I could call a taxi."

Curtis rubbed the back of his neck. "No. I do not prefer," he mimicked her accent. "I just don't want us being awkward around each other."

The pace of her heart began to ease. "I do not want that either."

"Good. I mean I know things between us are going to be strained. We shouldn't have acted like horny teenagers and let that night at Carlos' wedding get so out of hand. We're adults who share many of the same people in our lives. We need to get along."

His words had sliced into her heart. They were said so matter of face, as though he'd never considered them as more than a one night item.

She agreed, for the most part, that they needed to get along, they did share a great deal of people in their lives. But she certainly didn't want him to think that their time together had been wasted. She could fix this all with one statement. *I'm pregnant!* And she could risk him throwing her over the balcony too.

No. He needed to be okay with her before she told him she was carrying his baby. Even if he never loved her, which she hoped he would, she wanted him to like her. And no matter what he was saying she wasn't quite convinced he did.

CHAPTER 13

*C*urtis backed up as the grill flamed. The hair on the back of his hands might have caught the last flame that shot out from the grill, which could certainly use a cleaning.

At this point, there was enough of a crust on the steak he didn't know if the inside was bloody or overcooked. All he knew was the French heiress that broke his heart was standing only feet from him staring off into the woods from his balcony, nursing a glass of water.

Something was different about her, but he couldn't peg it. But wasn't that the way with women? They didn't actually want to tell you what was on their minds, but they sure as hell wanted you to suffer trying to figure it out. Well, he thought as he pulled the lonely steak from the grill, he didn't care.

There was nothing Simone Pierpont could be thinking that had any effect on him. He had his home. He had his job. And by God, he was going to keep his sanity.

He watched her as she lifted her hand to her hair and brushed her fingers through it. Even with her mind preoccupied, she was graceful.

What could she ever have seen in him, he wondered. He didn't wear suits, or have a Rolex watch. Before he met her, the only boat he'd been on, besides his father's fishing boat, was a river boat down from down town to Opry Land. The thought made him laugh. What would she think of that?

He pulled the stake off the grill and slid it onto a plate. "C'mon. I'll cut this up and we'll have a salad. Then if we're still hungry I'll hit a *Ben and Jerry's* on the way out to Zach and Regan's."

She smiled, but she didn't laugh. This much he knew, if she was humored, or even pretending to be, she'd toss that raven hair behind her shoulder with a flick of her wrist and roll her head back with a laugh. She did neither. Oh, something happened to her to make her leave the posh life she'd been used to and take some clerical job. There was a great amount of certainty that she wouldn't tell him why she'd moved to Nashville, but he figured he could get Zach to spill it.

Simone followed him inside.

She set her water glass on the table. "What can I do to help?"

Where did he begin? She could let go of the grip she had on his heart for starters. Instead, he handed her the bag of premixed salad. "Just throw some on plates."

As he turned to reach for a knife out of the drawer she reached above him to the cupboard where he kept his plates. Their bodies brushed against each other's. He'd been so close he felt her breath hitch, but she hadn't moved back, and neither did he.

He couldn't risk hurting again, but what did it matter? She'd be gone soon, no matter what she said. Simone would never live in Nashville and work for a clinic forever.

But he already hurt having her so near, smelling her scent, feeling her breath on his cheek.

Curtis rested his hand on her hip, just to steady each of them. When he looked at her, her eyes were closed. Was she taking in the moment too? They were touching. There was heat.

He could see the pulse in her neck beating rapidly. It would be easy to drop his head and kiss her. Just kiss her senseless until they wound up in a tangled mess on the floor as they had months ago.

But when Simone opened her eyes there was fear in them. That seemed more normal. She probably thought he was just some common man she could play with when she was in town.

Curtis shoved past her, took the knife out of the drawer, and stepped back. He wasn't going to make the same mistake twice.

The steak was cooked to his liking, but Simone hadn't touched hers. She'd picked at her salad, and drank three more glasses of water. On her third yawn, at only seven-forty-five, he decided to head toward his sister's house and take her home.

CURTIS NAVIGATED THE DIRT ROAD THAT LED TO HIS SISTER'S house. The ride had been too quiet. Though he had only his brief time with Simone, he knew that her recent bouts of silence weren't normal. He couldn't take it any longer. He had to talk.

"Cynthia really likes working at the clinic. Marsha is nice too." He thought he sounded pathetic.

"It will be a nice change of pace in my life. I am done with teas and dinners in fancy hotels schmoozing the money hungry hounds. Maybe I can do some good somewhere."

He'd opened a can of worms. "Most people want the schmoozing life you have."

She chuckled and that was more like Simone, especially when she flipped her hair over her shoulder.

Turning to him, she angled her head, which he was sure had been practiced a million times to show her good side.

"You told me, when we were together," she said and her tone softened, "that you hated dressing up and having to go to fundraisers for the hospital."

"Can't say that's wrong. I usually end up in the corner all

night drinking too many drinks served on trays." Not unlike the charity work he'd done at Carlos' weddings.

"Then, perhaps even only a little, you understand."

"I understand just that little part. But c'mon, you'd rather be here," he raised his hands to encompass all of Nashville as he saw it in his mind, "than on a jet flying to Spain for the weekend, or heading up to the Queen's for a polo match."

She stifled the next giggle. "I have never been to the Queen's." She let out a long sigh. "This is what I want." She raised her hands in the same manner as he had, only there was poise to it. But then she set them back in her lap and her fingers gripped all together until her knuckles were white. "Now all I have to do is secure a place to live and ensure I can pay for the lease on my car."

Worry flashed in her eyes. Something didn't match up. How was it that Simone was worried about paying for things? The thought of Cynthia giving her uniforms didn't settle with him either. Then he reminded himself he wasn't supposed to care. She wasn't his problem.

It struck him that he should just pull to the side of the road and see if she could find her own way back to Zach and Regan's house. That would be fitting. He'd had to do that from the middle of the fricking ocean.

His fingers tensed around the steering wheel as they had earlier as he'd driven around town, and he forced himself to relax. That was over. He needed to move on and forget about it. Without letting out the laugh that brewed inside of him the thought about the day some little kid would throw up on Simone at work. Even the office personnel didn't always escape the patients. That would certainly send her packing to Paris.

CHAPTER 14

Zach's office on the front of the house was illuminated as he parked the truck in the circular drive in front of the house. Good. He'd have to answer some questions since Curtis had driven all the way out there to drop off the Parisian princess, and she really hadn't given him more information than she didn't like stuffy parties.

She reached for the bag with the scrubs she'd gotten from Cynthia and climbed out of his truck. Curtis watched her move quickly as though she wanted to escape. "Thank you for dinner and for driving me out here. It was very thoughtful of you."

Her prim and proper ways annoyed him. Maybe she should stay in Nashville long enough to inherit a twang, yeah, that would have her posh friends freaking out.

"My pleasure, ma'am." He lifted his hands toward his head and tipped his imaginary hat to her. She smiled and her perfect teeth sparkled in the dim light as the sun set beyond the trees. But still, her smile didn't reach her eyes.

"I'll walk in with you. I wanted to talk to Zach for a minute."

Simone nodded, shut the door to the truck, and led him into the house.

Zach stood in the doorway of his office. "I didn't expect to see the two of you together." His eyebrows raised and Curtis shook his head. The slightest sign of a smile on Zach's face had Curtis itching to remove it.

Simone stepped forward to Zach, and kissed him on the cheek. "You were always watching out for me."

"It always seemed to be my job," Zach smiled down at her.

"I'm going to head to bed." She turned back to Curtis. "Thank you again for the ride."

"Sure." Both men watched her ascend the stairs and when her bedroom door shut, Curtis looked at Zach. "Pour me a drink and let's talk."

Curtis closed the door to Zach's office as Zach poured him a brandy. As soon as Zach handed it to him he threw it back and let it warm his throat.

Zach watched carefully. "She's driven you to drink."

"On more than one occasion." And that had been the truest statement of the night.

Zach secured the lid on the brandy and set it high on the shelf. "Regan said she went job hunting with Cynthia. How'd she end up with you?"

Curtis shrugged his shoulders and fell into the couch below him. He kicked his feet up on the coffee table and rested his head back. "Can you believe she got a job at the clinic?"

Zach didn't comment right away. He sipped his brandy, and then took the seat across from Curtis. "Simone has a job?"

Curtis dropped his feet to the floor. "Not only does she have a job, she works in a federally funded clinic. When I headed over to Cynthia's today she was there trying on scrubs Cynthia was giving her."

"She has a job and a bag of hand-me-downs?"

Curtis threw his hands in the air. "Exactly."

Zach leaned back in his chair. "She must be more pissed at her father than I thought she was."

"I was hoping you shed some light on that. What's up with her?"

This time Zach shrugged. "I flew her here. She called me two days before Carlos and Madeline's wedding and said she needed to be here, in Nashville. She needed a place to stay for a while, and she said she wanted to be on her own. It's not the first time she's said she's going to be independent, but she's never followed through, not this far at least."

"So she's done this before? Left all the glitz and glory of high society?" He waved his hand in the air. It made him feel better to think that she was making it all up. It would be short lived after all and that was what Curtis needed. He'd like it if he could show up to Cynthia's house for dinner whenever he wanted and not have to see Simone there, and Cynthia wouldn't be sending him away at night.

"She's tried to do this before. But she always had something set up with people in her father's industry." A look of concern washed over Zach's face and he reached for this brandy. "In fact, now that I think about it, the first time I met Michael Hamilton on our first build together, she introduced us."

Curtis watched his brother-in-law's jaw clench.

"You don't think Simone was involved with that woman-beating bastard do you?"

Zach shook his head. "No. She was as uncomfortable with him as I was. But that was how she thought she'd find independence. By getting involved with others like her father. That never worked out in her benefit."

Curtis didn't like the way it sounded at all. If she was so used to the power and the men with it, why come to the one place where no one had power like that. Why move to Nashville to mess with his mind. If she like power, prestige, and poise she'd come to the wrong place. Curtis had none of that.

"On the way here she said she was going to find a place to live and needed to pay for her lease on her car."

Zach finally drank down his brandy and looked at Curtis. "I have a tele-conference with her father at the end of the week. I'll ask him what she's up to."

"Good."

A smile formed on Zach's lips. "But at least the two of you are talking."

Curtis shook his head. "Don't go there," he said as he stood. "I think I walked into some trap today when I headed to Cynthia's. She left for a date, dropping Simone right into my care. That wasn't my idea of fun."

"So you just brought her back out here?"

The heat in the room was rising and Curtis rubbed the back of his neck. "Well, no. I offered to take her to dinner."

Zach was obviously trying to hide the smirk on his face again. "And what fancy place did she choose?"

Curtis rested his arms on his knees and leaned in toward Zach. "She didn't choose anything. Instead, she fell asleep in the truck and I took her to my place. I had one steak in the fridge and we shared it." He thought better of it. "Well, I ate it and she picked at a salad." Curtis shook his head again. "I've been a doctor long enough to know something is bothering her and it's affecting her. It's eating her up inside. She's not talking as much as I've heard you say she does." That forced a laugh from Zach. "She's not eating, isn't drinking, and she just looks plain scared. Whatever reason she's in Nashville, it's making her sick."

"For not wanting to pay attention to someone you're sure paying a lot of attention."

Curtis leaned back on the couch. "It's in the job, that's all. But if she doesn't calm down something is going to happen to her. I'm saying that since you're her friend and all."

"Not because you care."

Now he'd really like to knock that smirk off Zach's face. "Might have cared more if you hadn't had to send for me and buy me clothes just to get off the damn yacht."

"I'd do it again if I had to."

"You'll never have to." There was no way he was getting played again. From now on he'd be treading very carefully around Simone, especially since he knew getting involved with her was like swimming with the sharks.

Curtis stood. "Anyway, let me know what you find out. Now my curiosity is piqued."

"I'll look into it."

Curtis moved toward the office door and opened it.

Zach stood from his seat. "Curtis, thanks for taking care of her. She's very important to me, a sister if you will."

He gave his brother-in-law a nod and walked out of the house and to his truck. As he turned around in the drive he could see Simone's bedroom light turn off. He let out a long breath. Yeah, he'd take care of her no matter what. She seemed to be very important to him too.

CHAPTER 15

*S*imone stumbled down the stairs at six o'clock and the sun was already too bright. She wished she'd had the luxury she'd had her whole life, to stay in bed as long as she wanted. To stretch, yawn, and no matter what time you made it into the kitchen there was breakfast waiting for you.

But today she started her new life without the aid of anyone else. There was some merit to feeling totally unprepared for the day. She could do this. Everyone else in the world did it. However, morning sickness wasn't helping her along.

When she turned the corner into the kitchen, Zach was standing over the sink finishing his cup of coffee.

"Bon matin, belle."

She wrapped her head around his words and with a slow nod said, "Mornin'."

Zach laughed as he rinsed out his cup. "All right. That's better, a bit more Southern. I'll know you've been transformed when you give me a good *y'all.*"

Simone shuffled around him and found the loaf of bread tucked in the cabinet. She took out a slice and dropped it into the toaster, all the while knowing Zach was watching her every move with great enjoyment. He always was a morning person and she loathed that about him.

"So today is your first day, huh?"

Simone simply nodded.

"Do you want a ride?"

She shook her head.

"Are you feeling okay?"

She finally looked up, her eyelids heavy. "*Idiot!* Do not tease me. You know I despise mornings."

"*Excusez-moi.*" He was laughing at her. That should have been comfortable. There had been many times in her life that her dearest friend, this *idiot*, had laughed at her—with her, but now she wasn't laughing.

"I have to get ready." She walked out of the kitchen.

"What about your toast?" he called after her, but she kept walking.

An hour later when she'd walked back down to the kitchen, her toast was on a plate smeared with strawberry jelly. A glass of orange juice sat next to it. A note in Zach's handwriting read, *Let's try this again. Good morning, beautiful. Have a nice day on your first day of work. Love, The Idiot.*

This time she laughed.

"He's worried about you." Regan's voice broke the silence in the kitchen.

Simone looked up to see her seated at the table, a sleeping Tyler rested in her arms. Simone picked up her plate and the glass and walked to the table.

"He is already sleeping?" She motioned toward Tyler.

"Well he's been up since four."

"I never heard him." Simone sat down and kept her eyes on the precious boy.

"We have a routine. And I think today that routine has mama laying down for a nap with him later." Regan brushed her hand gently over his head.

Simone watched the small gestures, and her heart ached in her chest. If she didn't enlist Curtis' help, and soon, she wouldn't have moments like the one she was witnessing. No, she'd have to put the baby into care right away so she could afford to feed them both.

The very thought made her sick and Regan noticed. "Zach says you're not feeling well."

"I am just nervous."

Regan gave her a reassuring smile, and then she reached across the table and laid her hand gently atop Simone's. "I'm very proud of you. For whatever reason you came to live with us and decided to take your life into your own hands, I think that was a blessing. I know how hard it is to do that, but I also know the rewards." She looked down at Tyler then back up at Simone. "You're going to do great."

Simone swallowed hard. Perhaps Regan knew more than she was letting on.

ONE THING WAS FOR SURE, SIMONE PIERPONT HAD NEVER HAD TO battle morning commute traffic. There were certainly reasons to have a driver.

She pulled up in front of the clinic ten minutes late. She parked her car, grabbed her paperwork, and hurried inside. Marsha was waiting for her in the lobby.

"I thought you'd changed your mind," she said sternly with her arms crossed in front of her.

"I was caught in traffic. I am sorry. I will make sure I make more time tomorrow."

Marsha nodded and turned to go into the clinic. Simone followed.

One thing she could say for sure was that the scrubs she'd gotten from Cynthia were certainly comfortable. For the first time in her life she didn't feel confined. She'd pulled her hair back into a ponytail and wore her smallest diamond earrings. Perhaps no one would notice such a small bit of glamour.

As they walked to Marsha's office Simone caught sight of Cynthia. She waved and Cynthia gave her a nod, but was already hurrying past to take care of a patient.

A half our later Simone was in her own office, with another woman, learning the ins and outs of her data entry job. The work was simple. Input, input, input, but nerve wracking at the same time.

The other woman wasn't much help when it came to answering questions, but she'd do it each time with an enormous sigh, her hands then dropping heavily onto her desk, and a huge push off for the chair she sat in to roll toward Simone. She never once stood up and walked over to her. It was obvious Simone wasn't making a new friend. But that didn't matter. She had a job, and she was going to keep it—this was the life.

After three hours, Simone realized her cheeks hurt from smiling. She was working. She was making her own living doing a job she'd had to learn from someone who was even more stubborn than her father.

She'd had to ask questions, make mistakes, and fix them. It might not mean much to her father, but it did to Simone.

CHAPTER 16

*S*imone took a long bubble bath the moment she'd gotten home. She'd only had a few moments to speak to Cynthia during her entire day. She'd worked her eight hours, eaten lunch from the vending machines, and drank stale, cold coffee. She'd never have thought it would be the best day of her life.

But she was exhausted.

As she lounged in her yoga pants and her wet hair piled high on her head, she put cream on her face and arms and smiled at herself in the mirror. Would her own mother even recognize her?

"Simone! Simone, where are you?" Zach's voice bellowed through the hallway and it was filled with anger. "Simone!"

She jumped up and ran to the door. He was right on the other side ready to grab the handle as she pulled it open.

"Zachary, what is the matter?"

"What is going on?" His teeth were gritted and his cheeks bright red.

"I beg your pardon." Her voice strained as he pushed past her.

"I've been trying to call you all day long. Why don't you answer your phone?"

She swallowed hard. "I do not have a phone."

"And why is that? Not once in your life have you not had that phone within an inch of your hand."

She folded her arms. "What is your problem?"

"My problem?" Zach paced the room then ran his fingers through his hair. "I had a very heated discussion with your father today. That is my problem."

He moved to the window as if he were going to open it, but then thought better about it knowing it was only going to let in the humidity and make the air in the room even thicker, for which she was thankful. Instead, he turned around and stared at her. "You're cut off? You've been cut off from Pierpont Oil?"

The air in her lungs and the pride that had swelled in her chest deflated. She shut the door and turned to him.

"My father has said I am no longer his daughter."

Zach rubbed his forehead. "What the hell did you do?"

She stood there speechless, her mouth open. How could she possibly answer him?

Instead she pushed back her shoulders and jaunted out her chin. "How dare you talk to me like that."

"Oh, you're his princess. You know it. You'd have had to do something pretty bad to get him to be that mad so that he's *actually* cut you off."

"He did not tell you? He did not want to share with you why he thinks I am so unfit to represent his name?"

"God, Simone." He threw his hands in the air. "What did you do?"

She pursed her lips, and then let her arms fall. She sure as hell wasn't going to let Zachary Benson bully her into giving up her secrets. They weren't for him to hear—not yet.

"My father is just an obstinate ass. He thinks he can push people around with his money and his power. Well I for one am done with how he treats people."

"But, Simone, he loves you."

She shook her head. "He loves his money and his power. He has never loved me." And having seen the inner dynamics of the Keller family she knew that statement was true. Never, in her entire life, had her father looked at her the way Zach looked at Tyler, or Carlos looked at his children.

Zach took a step toward her. "Why did he do this?"

"He's hateful."

"No, he's a father." He reached for her. "What about your mother? She has no opinion on this?"

Simone jerked back. "Oh, what would she care? She is married and being spoiled by her new young husband. They are God knows where on an extended honeymoon and then she has purchased a house in France to spend all her new husband's money in. She has no time for me."

His eyes softened. "I haven't heard him this mad since Michael Hamilton walked away from our business deal."

"Oh, well that tells you where his priorities are. He almost stopped doing business with you over that, and the man beat and nearly killed your wife. Why would anything I did be different? I have hurt his pride. I've embarrassed him."

"But what did you do?"

She bit the inside of her cheek. "I cannot believe he did not tell you."

"Does this have to do with leaving Curtis on the yacht?"

Now she turned from him. It had everything to do with leaving Curtis on the yacht.

"Oh, Simone." He turned her toward him, took hands in his and held them. "I will help you no matter what you need. But you have to tell me what happened. You have to tell me why you left him and then chose to come here. Your father wouldn't say more than he didn't want to speak of you. If you're in some kind of trouble you need to tell me."

Simone pulled her hands back. "You would step in to save me? Poor Simone cannot take care of herself."

Zach held his hands up defensively. "I didn't say that."

"No one thinks I can take care of myself. I am just some rich girl who needs her daddy. But I do not need his money."

Zach scrubbed his hand over his face. "Honey, something happened. Your father has been mad before, but this is…"

"This is nothing. You need not worry." She sucked in a deep breath and pushed her shoulders back. "I will pay you back for flying me here. I appreciate your generosity. I have a job and I will be finding myself a place to live."

"Oh, that's just silly. You live here."

She shook her head. "I am intruding here. And if you are going to be yelling at me like a child I do not belong here."

"Simone." Zach moved to her and pulled her into his arms. "You're like my sister. I would do anything for you."

Simone stepped back. "Then trust me. I have done what I need to do and when it is time I will tell you why my father has pushed me away. But until then I need you to love me, trust me, and support my decisions."

Zach kissed her on the forehead. "Okay. I'll let you be. But Regan and I are here for you. Open up to us."

"I will, in time."

CHAPTER 17

Simone's first week of work had been successful. Simone had quickly learned the quickest route to work to avoid traffic. She knew she needed to pack a few snacks to keep her stomach calm, and she hated to admit that she thoroughly enjoyed Cynthia's company.

They sat together at the picnic table behind the clinic on Cynthia's dinner break from the hospital. She'd confided in Simone that if you didn't leave on your break you'd never get to eat.

"How do you juggle two jobs?" Simone asked as she bit into her apple.

"You manage. I suppose if I had a family it would be harder, but it's just me."

"Do you ever want to get married?"

Cynthia shrugged her shoulder. "I don't know. Seems like a lot of work."

They'd forged quite a friendship in the past week. Or at least that's what Simone thought it was. Her only true friend had been Zach, so she wasn't quite sure this was an honest friendship. But there was a nagging question that needed to be addressed and she figured now was as good a time as any to dive into Cynthia's life with Curtis.

"Don't you and Curtis ever plan to get married?"

Cynthia had just taken a drink of her green Naked juice when Simone asked. That had been a mistake. A moment later Cynthia was spitting it out on the ground as she laughed.

"Curtis? Me? Oh you have to be kidding."

"But that night at his parents' house you were kissing him on the porch. He showed up to your house for dinner. It seems to me you are very close."

Cynthia wiped her mouth with the back of her hand. "We are close. As close as two people can be, but I don't have any plans to spend my life with Curtis Keller."

"Why not?" It had almost come out as an accusation. Wasn't he good enough for her?

"Are you serious?"

Simone didn't like being played. Of course she was serious. What could possibly be wrong with the man that would make Cynthia not want to spend her life with him?

Not knowing what else to say Simone simply nodded hoping Cynthia would elaborate.

"Curtis works too many hours. His job is more important than anything else in his life. He's not married to a woman, he's married to the hospital. Next comes his family. But beyond that, he doesn't want me. He wants you."

This time it was Simone that choked on her apple. "Me?"

"Oh, you broke his heart into a million pieces, and he isn't going to forget that. And I'll admit, it might have cost you a chance with him forever." That phrase alone stabbed Simone right in the heart. Cynthia continued. "He doesn't forgive. If you do him wrong you might as well know you're going to pay for it forever. But you have his heart, darlin'. The poor man is smitten with you."

Well what was she supposed to say to that? Perhaps she could just tell him about the baby and he'd be welcoming and drop on one knee. But Cynthia did make it a point to tell her he didn't forgive. And what she'd done to him was unforgivable.

She needed to keep working to prove to him—and the rest of the world—that she was able to change.

Sitting there with her hair pulled up, in another pair of scrubs that Cynthia had given her, a pair of comfortable walking shoes on her feet, and a lunch packed in a bag, she knew she was doing the right thing. Her posh life was surely missed, but she was enjoying the freedom of having nothing.

As Cynthia gathered her trash, Sam opened the door and walked out of the clinic. Simone watched as Cynthia's eyes lit up.

"Hey, tall and handsome," Cynthia cranked her neck to look up at him.

"Hey."

Simone smiled. He was a man of very few words, but she'd seen him with his patients, his compassion and understanding was unrivaled.

Cynthia stood. Next to the man she gazed upon, she was dwarfed by his enormous size, but that didn't seem to bother her. Simone liked men to be eye to eye with her. It kept the playing field even.

"So, you taking me out this weekend?" Cynthia asked as she walked toward the trash can and tossed in her trash.

"Sure."

"I want to go dancing." She turned and looked at Simone. "Want to go dancing?"

"Me?" Simone's voice shot up. "Oh, I don't suppose I can dance the way you do."

"C'mon, it'd be fun." Cynthia shifted her eyes back to Sam. "We'll get her a date and boot-scoot-boogy." She nudged him with her elbow, but Simone didn't miss the glance she'd taken at his butt. "Gotta get back. See you two around."

They watched as Cynthia jogged back toward the hospital and then Sam sat down.

It was silent between them, but it wasn't awkward. Simone appreciated that. She'd been forced small talk her entire life, but she'd never taken the time to enjoy silence.

Sam pulled a soda from the front pocket of his scrubs and pulled the top open. He took a long, loud sip and set it back on the table.

"You still looking for a place to live?" he asked.

Simone hadn't been prepared for him to speak to her and she couldn't help but answer his question with an unintelligent, "Huh?" Oh, her mother would have choked and her father would have given her an evil look.

"My roommate moved out and I'm lookin' for a new one."

"Me?"

He picked up his soda and took another sip as he nodded.

It hadn't been something she'd considered, sharing an apartment with someone else, let alone a man she didn't know. But the thought was intriguing, and it would help her save money.

Sam seemed safe, kind, and it was sure generous of him to think of her when he'd told her about the opening. It might be just the right move. Besides, Cynthia was comfortable with him, and she'd been plenty comfortable with Curtis, so Sam must be a good guy.

"You know, I think that sounds lovely."

"Lovely?" He hit his chest as he let out a silent burp, which had Simone on the edge of laughter. The people she spent time with now certainly were different than the people she'd been surrounded by her entire life. Sam nodded again. "You sure talk fancy."

"I am sorry."

"Sorry? For something like talking pretty?" He huffed. "That's silly."

Simone stared at him dumbfounded by his comment and then she relaxed back and watched him. He was right. It was silly. In fact, everything she'd ever held dear suddenly seemed silly.

How was it that she'd been taught every fancy manner there was and yet she thought his silent burp had been almost endearing?

She wanted to laugh, skip, run through the yard and just scream. Things were different and she loved it. Thank goodness Curtis Keller happened into her life and made her face life outside the box in which she'd been shut into. She felt free.

"Sam, I think I would love to be your roommate. When can I move in?"

"As soon as you want to."

"Wonderful." She stood and gathered her trash. "I will plan to move in this weekend. You do not by chance have an extra bed do you?"

He shook his head. "I have a blow up mattress if that'll help."

This time she did laugh. How ridiculous was that? Wonderful and ridiculous. "That should be fine."

As she passed by him she stopped and kissed his unshaven cheek. "Thank you."

"Sure."

Everything was wonderful. Life was plentiful, even without money. Time was hers to make of it as she wanted. Could it get any better?

Well, sure it could. If Curtis Keller would sweep her off her feet and ask her to marry him and live happily ever after, that would make it better. However, nothing could stop her from being giddy with happiness.

As she opened the door to the clinic she saw the woman she'd seen the first day Cynthia had brought her in to meet Marsha. She thought quickly for a name. Regina. This time she had a black eye and her arm was in a sling.

The air of happiness whooshed out of her lungs and she was

quickly reminded that life wasn't just some grand yacht ride in the sun. People were hurt, sad, miserable, and abused. Simone slid her hand over her stomach. What was she thinking bringing a baby into such a cruel world?

CHAPTER 18

*S*imone walked through the clinic and to the restroom. She shut the door to the stall and pressed her fingers to her eyes. Seeing Regina battered and abused, again, had her emotions on a roller coaster ride. No woman deserved that.

She thought about Regan. Zach had been very candid when he told her about her father's business associate Michael Hamilton, whom had nearly beaten Regan to death when he'd tried to rid himself of her and marry another woman. What made men do such things? Certainly, Curtis couldn't find it in his heart to be so horrible, could he? She rested her hands on her stomach feeling the energy from her child.

Regan had another child, she'd given that child up for adoption when she'd been attacked. When Zach had learned of the baby he'd called Simone, and as a best friend would do, he'd confided in her.

Simone couldn't help but wonder why Regina didn't run.

Not all men were so evil. Zachary, of course, would never hurt a woman. And having been around Regan's brother's and father, Simone knew she'd be safe if she could just stay among them. When Curtis learned of the baby he'd protect them, that part she was sure of.

She thought about Sam. She was about to put her life in his hands as well. They'd be living in the same place, sharing an address, having access to each other all the time. Could he become violent?

She certainly didn't want to think he could.

When she'd composed herself, she washed her hands and wiped her eyes. Working in an environment where people had to care for others was going to be a challenge. Never in her life, no matter how many large checks she'd seen her father pass to organizations, had she seen the need that was out there. Only humanity could save some of the people who walked through the doors of the clinic.

Regina was near the water cooler when Simone walked toward her office. She had the baby she'd carried the other day on her hip and tried to juggle the glass of water while her other arm was in a sling.

Simone hurried to her. "Let me get that for you."

"Thanks." Her voice was soft.

"Regina, correct?"

"I like your accent." Regina smiled. "How'd you know my name?"

"My friend Cynthia is one of the nurses here. I remember her talking to you."

Regina nodded. "Yeah, she's nice to us."

"Where would you like me to take this?" She held the glass of water in her hand.

"Over there." Regina pointed to a bed behind a curtain. "They're making me stay. The cops arrested Darius' ass, but I think Sam is making excuses to keep me here."

"Sam?"

"Yeah, that big nurse. He always tells me if Darius lays a hand on me again he'll kill him."

Simone looked out the window where the giant of a man sipped his soda. She smiled. He'd be safe to live with.

She followed Regina to the curtained off area and set the water on the nightstand next to the bed.

"Thanks. Would you mind holding him for a minute?" Regina turned toward Simone with the baby asleep against her shoulder. "He's getting so heavy."

Simone reached her arms out and took the baby, but it was the most awkward of feelings. It was completely unnatural.

"How old is he?"

"Six months." Regina sat down on the bed and kicked her feet up. "It's hard to take care of him and try and find work. I can't leave him with Darius, obviously." She nodded to her arm.

"What kind of work do you do?"

"Nothing fancy. My last job, I cleaned hotel rooms."

Simone nodded. Her mind was wrapping around being a single mother who had no options for her child. What was she going to do with her own child when she had to go to work to support them?

Regina adjusted on the bed. "You doin' okay? Your face is pale."

"I'm fine." Simone shifted the baby on her shoulder. "What will you do now? They certainly will not keep him in jail for long."

"If I could afford a place to live, and had a job where I could take my baby, I'd make sure we had a decent life. He deserves that."

Simone listened to this woman who was desperately in need of help to make a better life for herself and her son. How did a woman do that when there was a man who wanted to hurt her?

"What will you do if you do not get a job?"

Regina shrugged. "I've pawned all my grandma's jewelry. Any money I did have Darius spent it on booze."

The curtain moved and Marsha stood there looking at Simone. "You'd best get back to work."

"Yes, sorry." She passed the baby back to Regina.

"Thanks for helpin' me out."

"It was my pleasure." She gave her a smile and went back to her desk, thankful she had a job—for now.

The rest of the day dragged on. She knew Regina and her son were still in the clinic. The pile on her desk kept growing, but her mind wasn't on her work. She kept thinking about the cost of food, rent, and daycare. How did anyone make it all work?

She combed her fingers through her ponytail and then absentmindedly she began to twist her earring between her fingers. It was an old habit. One her mother used to nag her about stopping. When she let go of her ear she instantly went back to the earring. She unclasped it and held it in her hand. Her father had given them to her for her sixteenth birthday. She'd worn them to work because she thought they were small and not fancy, but each earring was well over a karat. She took the other earring out and looked at them in her palm. Each earring would feed Regina and her son for a few weeks. She could afford diapers and maybe buy herself some time to get away from Darius.

Her mind began brewing with ideas. She knew a lot of people in Nashville, a lot of people with businesses and means to help others. Zach. Zach offered his employees daycare for their children. She'd remembered her father speaking ill of the idea. But now she saw the glory in it.

She stood from her desk and hurried out to the clinic floor. Regina was standing with Sam, who was loading up her diaper bag with diapers from the storage closet.

"Are you leaving?" Simone's voice was fast and her heart rate quickened.

"Yeah, your boss says I can't stay any longer."

Simone nodded as Sam handed her back her bag. "You come back here if he comes home. You understand?" Sam asked.

"Yes. I'll come back."

He gave her a nod and walked away.

Simone squeezed her hand tight, the earrings dug into her skin. "Here." She opened Regina's hand that wrapped around her son. She slid the earrings into her palm and closed her fingers around them. "You use these and feed you and your baby. If you need to get a hotel room, use them for that. Then, I want you to call me in the morning, here at the clinic. I think I can get you a job with daycare."

Regina stood before her, her eyes wide and mouth open. "Why you bein' so nice to me?"

"Every mother deserves to protect herself and her baby. You need to protect yourself."

"And you're helping me?"

"This is all I can do."

Tears were forming in Regina's eyes. "Thank you. You have the kindest heart."

That nearly had Simone's knees buckling beneath her. No one had ever told her she was kind.

"You call me in the morning."

"I'll do that." Regina smiled and batted away the tears. "Thank you. God bless you."

CHAPTER 19

*C*ynthia sat at the nurses' station leaned back in her chair when Curtis walked by. The smug smile on her lips had him stop. He realized he was smiling too just looking at her sitting there as if she was up to something.

"You have something on your face."

She raised her eyebrows. "Do I?"

"Yeah, a grin that says you're up to no good."

She crossed her legs and bounced her foot which adorned bright pink Nikes. "Oh, well I'm never up to any good. But that little princess of yours is."

"Little, what…oh." He leaned over the counter. "What did she do now? Abandon that job already?"

"Oh, ye of little faith." Cynthia moved in closer to him and rested her arms on the counter as well. "I'll tell you what she did if you promise to go dancing on Saturday."

"Dancing?" Cynthia nodded and he shook his head. "If I remember right I can't keep up with you. But fine. I'll go dancing. Now tell me what did she do?"

Simone paced in Zach's office. She hadn't had reason to visit him at work in months, and when she'd shown up with her hair piled atop her head, her makeup worn off, and in scrubs of all things, his assistant Mary Ellen told her she'd almost called security.

Other times she'd have sat on his desk and crossed her tan legs so that it would have been the first thing he'd see, even though he'd never looked at her legs in all the years she'd known him. He was absolutely the only man who looked her in the eye.

She sat down on the leather couch and gripped her hands together to keep them from shaking. Why was she so nervous? This was Zachary.

It had taken him twenty minutes to make it back to his office after his meeting.

"I swear I just witnessed you bite your nails," he said from the doorway.

"*Tais-toi!*" She stood up and wiped her palms on the legs of her pants. "I need help."

Zach quickly shut the office door and walked to her. He reached for her arms and looked her over. "Are you okay? What happened?"

"I need you to hire someone."

Zach narrowed his eyes on her. "You need me to hire someone?" He shook his head and let loose a laugh that had her temper fume.

"I need you."

"I offered you a job. And you turned me down." He let go of her arms, walked to his desk, and began to go through the papers that lay on it.

"It is not for me. Will you listen to me?"

Zach looked up from the papers he shuffled. "Okay. Who do you want me to hire?"

Simone swallowed hard. "Her name is Regina. She needs a full time job. She is comfortable in housekeeping, and she needs to put her son in daycare."

He watched her carefully before folding his arms. "What has gotten into you?"

"I am asking for help. If you are not going to help me then I will ask someone else. You are not the only contact I have in this city."

Zach stepped around from behind his desk. "Now calm down."

"Are you going to help me?"

"I've never seen this side to you. It's endearing."

"I need an answer," she pleaded. How could she be so desperate for someone else's well-being?

Zach took her hands in his. "I'll alert personnel that she'll be by to fill out an application."

"Oh, thank you." Simone wrapped her arms around his neck. "You do not know what this means to me."

When she took a step back, he was smiling wide. "I'm proud of you."

"No reason to be. I don't think I have been a very good person in my life."

"You've always been a wonderful person. You're just now finding out what it is to be humane."

She wasn't sure that was in any way a compliment, but she couldn't argue with him. It had felt good to give her earrings to Regina and even better to know her son would be well looked after. Six months ago she would have looked down on the woman. Then again, she'd never have even had the pleasure to have met her had she not made the biggest mistake of her life and left Curtis on that yacht.

Regina had called first thing in the morning and Simone shared with her the information she had from Zach. There was a

94

joy in Regina's voice she'd never heard in anyone else's voice before. She sincerely appreciated the helping hand.

The pile on her desk dwindled before lunch, and when she stood up to take her lunch she was surprised to find Curtis standing in her doorway.

"I did not know you were here." She tried to remain calm around him, but her body temperature rose just having him a few feet away.

"I never would have thought you could type that fast."

She narrowed her eyes on him. "How long have you been there?"

"Long enough." He stepped into her office and from behind his back he pulled out a potted plant and handed it to her. "I thought this would look nice on your desk."

Simone felt tears sting her eyes. Why couldn't she keep her emotions in tact? "You brought me a plant for my desk?"

"Yeah," he said as he sat it on the corner of the desk and took a step back toward the door. "Cynthia also told me what you did for your patient. Well for the clinic's patient."

"Cynthia? How did she..."

"Sam."

She hadn't realized anyone had seen her do that.

Curtis took a step back. "My sister also called me this morning and told me that you'd arranged a job for the woman with Zach so that she'd have a job and daycare."

Simone dropped her shoulders. "I wish he had not said anything."

"He's proud of you."

"There should not be such compassion given to me for what I did."

"For helping someone? Why not?"

She shook her head. "Because it was the first time in my life that I have ever helped anyone, yet you and your family do it all the time."

He smiled wide. "You are as close to a sister as Zach has. As far as I'm concerned that makes you part of this family."

Simone sucked in a deep breath and sat down in the chair behind her. He'd included her in his family, even if just by association.

She focused on the gift he'd brought her and tried to steady her breathing so her voice would not shake. "Thank you for the plant."

"You're welcome." He tucked his thumbs into his front pockets. "I'd wanted to take you to lunch, but I have a meeting."

She was on the verge of a breakdown. Why was he doing this to her? Gifts, conversation, compliments and now even the thought that he'd wanted to take her out was threatening to send her running to the bathroom in joyful tears. "That was very thoughtful of you."

He took another step toward her. "I also heard you got yourself a place."

"Yes."

"And a roommate, huh?"

"It was quite unexpected."

He cleared his throat. "Seems as though the women in my life have taken to Sam the Giant Nurse."

The nickname made her laugh and she lowered her head to hide her smile. "He is a very nice man."

"Yeah, well he'd better be. I'm not too worried about Cynthia. She'll kick his ass if he hurts her."

Simone's jaw tightened. "I don't think he would do that."

"I don't think so either."

There was a raw nerve that his compassion for Cynthia struck, jealousy, maybe? "You care about her a lot, don't you?"

He nodded slowly, as if he were thinking about her. "I suppose it's like you and Zach. She's always got my back."

The comparison gave her hope. Sure she'd been giddy over Zachary Benson most her life, but it was only because he'd shown her kindheartedness when no one else would. She'd never turned his head, that much she knew was different between her and Cynthia. Cynthia had certainly turned Curtis' head. But if he was comparing their relationship to the one she had with Zachary, then Cynthia wasn't a threat at all.

"It also seems as though your new roommate's girlfriend has scammed me into going dancing this weekend."

Simone looked up at him. "And you are going?"

"I assume you are too?" She nodded and he smiled. "When are you moving in with Sam?" His voice shifted in pitch when he said his name.

"Saturday."

"Need some help?" A giddy flutter took over in her chest. This was a moment that could change her life.

"I only have a suitcase."

He stood there a moment longer, gave her a slow nod, and turned and left. He hadn't said goodbye and she took that as a good sign, as if they weren't parting ways.

She put her hand on her stomach. There was hope. Curtis Keller had brought her a gift and an invitation to pick her up for a date.

The need to laugh replaced the earlier desire to cry. She was happy that her co-worker wasn't in the room, because laugh she did. She laughed until she cried.

Money and prestige couldn't buy the kind of happiness she was feeling. This was going to work. If she kept her calm and made sure Curtis forgave her for what she'd done, she could ease him into learning about the baby.

The time was coming. Regan had announced her pregnancy. There was joy in that arrival. Perhaps it was time she was able to share in that joy with her own pending arrival.

But the laugher died down and she sat still for a moment. She needed to keep a level head. What if Cynthia was right and Curtis Keller refused to forgive her?

CHAPTER 20

Zach was up on Saturday morning dressed in a pair of jeans and a Benson, Benson, and Hart softball team T-shirt. He sipped his cup of coffee as he rested against the counter.

Simone would miss talking to him in the mornings, but now she wouldn't live countries away.

"Do you never sleep in?"

"Not on moving day."

She retrieved a mug from the cupboard and shifted her eyes to him. "Moving day?"

"You didn't think you were just going to sneak out did you? I have John Forrester's truck outside loaded up and ready to go."

"Loaded up?" She set the empty mug on the counter. "I only have one suitcase."

"Yeah, I know. But between John moving, my mother redecorating, and my wife's need to clean her closet out, that truck is now full of clothes, a bed, a dresser, lamps, and I don't know what else. I hope Sam's place has space. You're going to need it."

She thought her heart might burst. "They all did this for me?"

"They all love you, Simone."

There was no fighting back the tears now. They streamed down her cheek and she brushed them away as quickly as she could.

He reached for the dishtowel that had hung over the sink, handed it to her, and she wiped her eyes.

Zach chuckled. "In all my life I don't think I've ever seen you cry at the drop of a hat."

"This independence makes me a bit emotional."

Zach picked up his coffee and took a sip. "I talked to your father yesterday. He asked about you."

She wadded the towel in her hands. "And what did you tell him."

"I said you were doing great. I told him he'd be pleased with how you were getting along."

The circulation in her fingers was being cut off from the tension from the towel being wrapped around them. "Is that all?"

"Yes. He was very brief."

She nodded. It was certainly more than she'd ever expected. She unwrapped the towel from her hands and hung it back over the sink. "I am ready to go."

Zach nodded toward the empty coffee mug on the counter. "Don't you want some coffee?"

"No. I just want to get moving."

SIMONE FOUGHT EMOTIONS THAT THREATENED TO ATTACK HER between uncontrollable laughter and tears. The morning had been full of surprises already. Tyler had reached out for her and rested his head against her shoulder. Regan had cried when she'd left, even though she wasn't really going away. The truck filled with items that people were giving her to start her new life drove down the street in front of her.

The tears had started and stopped a number of times on the ten miles from her best friend's house to her new home. And that was where the biggest surprise of them all nearly stopped her heart.

Curtis sat on the steps of the building. When he saw her pull up, he stood, and when she stopped the car, he walked toward her.

Her breath was coming in rapid spurts, her heart beat an unnatural rhythm in her chest, and her mind was blank. She could see his blue eyes peering at her through the window, but she didn't make a move to get out of the car.

A moment later Curtis pulled open the door. "Were you just going to watch us move all this stuff, or are you planning on helping?"

Her voice still hid within her throat. He was absolutely the most handsome man she'd ever laid eyes on, and she'd had her fair share of male models and well taken care of men. Curtis was a bit rugged for her usual taste, but she'd long ago decided that she simply hadn't known her taste until that first moment he'd slipped his arm around her waist and pulled her in close to dance and Carlos' first wedding of the year.

His brows lifted and then lowered in concern. "Are you okay? You look as though you've been crying."

"This is all just a bit overwhelming—this whole week really. Your girlfriend gets me a job…"

"Not my girlfriend," he said with a grin.

Simone acknowledged with a nod. "Sam offers me a place to live, and I do not know him."

"He's a decent man. He won't hurt you. Are you worried about that?"

She couldn't say no, even though she didn't think he would. "It is just that I have never lived with a man."

"It's not like the two of you are going to be having sex in the kitchen." His lips pursed. "You're not are you?"

Heat rose in Simone's cheeks. "I most certainly am not." She pulled herself out of the car but was still pinned against it by Curtis who hadn't stepped back. "Is that what you think of me? You think I moved here to sleep my way around?"

Curtis reached his hand to her face and caressed her cheek with his thumb. "I didn't mean it to come out that way. I'm a little gun shy having you this close."

She was drowning in a sea of confusion. He wanted her, he didn't. He loved her, he loathed her. She couldn't get a grip on what was going on.

"Curtis, you are crowding me. I need to get inside."

His hand still lingered on her cheek. "I'm here to help." He bore a stare of warning and concern at her. "You hurt me, Simone. I've never hurt that bad in my life."

She dropped her gaze to the ground and he lifted her chin with his finger until she looked at him. "Curtis, I am sorry."

"I think you are. I want us to be friends. You mean the world to Zach and my sister. Now here you are intertwined into every aspect of my life." He let out a deep breath and lowered his forehead to hers. "You've changed. I don't know what it is, but you've changed."

She swallowed hard. How much did he know?

"I am more than the face of Pierpont Oil."

"I know. I didn't then, but I do now. You cemented that in my mind when you helped Regina."

"No woman with a child deserves that."

"You're right." He stepped back and looked at her. "I saw my sister nearly die at the hands of a man. I saw her heart break when she gave up her daughter. You saved Regina from all that. And if she keeps going on the path you set for her you will have saved her life."

Those damn tears broke free again and they rolled down her cheeks.

Curtis brushed them away. "It feels good to save a life, doesn't it?"

She could only nod. There were no words for his compassion.

He pulled her into his arms and held her until she'd composed herself.

"Curtis, thank you."

Zach pounded his fist on the hood of the car forcing them to jump apart. "I've successfully untied everything all by myself. Do you two think you could stop making out in the street long enough to help me move this stuff?"

Simone laughed against Curtis' chest. She'd never felt so taken care of in her entire life.

AFTER A MORNING SPENT WITH ZACH IN CONTROL OF coordinating everything, she understood better why he was so successful. She'd seen him dealing with men in suits at a meeting, but she now knew he could throw his weight around a work site just as well.

She'd heard every curse word Curtis knew and Zach's voice had risen to levels she'd never heard. But in the end, she had a bed, a dresser, a chair, a television, a closet full of clothes, and a place she called her own.

She stood in her new bedroom, which was the size of her closet in her father's home, and she smiled. Who would have ever thought she'd be so happy in such a small space.

"Have you ever slept on a waterbed?" Curtis leaned against the doorjamb.

"No, I certainly have not. I did not know that was what was in the truck." She let out a giggle.

"They can be fun." He winked at her and she looked away. As much as she wanted to eat up the charm, she couldn't just pull him in the room and roll on the bed. There was something he would certainly notice and he couldn't find out that way.

"I cannot believe Regan gave me all these clothes."

"Well you have to figure she's on baby number two, and I think they are far from done having babies. So this is part of her old life."

Simone turned from him so he couldn't see the fear she felt creep over her. "It was very nice of everyone."

Curtis touched her shoulder. "It's okay to be overwhelmed. You've never needed anyone before."

He was right she hadn't. It was hard to have to be humble.

He turned her around to him and held her against him, again. "You've gotten involved with the wrong family if you can't accept graciously."

She turned her head and rested it against his chest. "Am I involved with this family?"

"More than I thought I wanted you to be." She felt him suck in a breath and let it out slow. "I couldn't get you out of my head. No woman has ever done that to me before."

"I hurt you."

"More than anyone ever has." He brushed his lips across the top of her head. "Have you ever forgiven someone?"

"No."

"Me either, so I guess we're going to have to work around that." He chuckled. "Let's start with going out and dancing."

Simone stepped back and nodded. "I think I would like that."

"I'm going home and getting a shower. I'll pick you up at seven."

"I'll be ready."

He turned to leave the room and looked back at her. "Don't take this the wrong way, because it's going to come out sounding bad. But I like what Tennessee has done to you already. You're feeling like a real woman in my arms with those nice curves." He winked and walked away.

Simone fell to the bed. He'd noticed too much. She ran her hands over her stomach. It wouldn't be long before there would be no hiding it. Tonight had to win him over or his comment about not forgiving would force her back to France and she'd have to gravel at her father's feet. That wasn't an option.

CHAPTER 21

The best part about Simone's new wardrobe was that Regan, though still petite and small, was two sizes bigger than she was. She'd have lots of room for a while in her new clothes. There was a denim skirt, black sleeveless shirt with mother-of-pearl snaps, and a worn pair of boots.

Simone grinned at herself when she looked in the mirror. Though it was almost as if she'd dressed in a costume, she couldn't remember a time, even in her own clothes, that she'd looked better.

Sam knocked on her door. "You look good."

"Thanks. I have never worn boots like this before."

"Now you're Southern." He bit into the apple he held in his hand. "You're all moved in?"

"Yes. And thank you for offering to let me stay here. It was very kind of you."

Sam shrugged a shoulder as he took another bite of his apple. "I ain't here much. But as long as you're paying half the rent, stay as long as you want."

"Thank you, again."

"Oh, and I figure I'll stay at Cynthia's tonight. You can bring Curtis back if you want."

She'd never contemplated *not* bringing a man back home for the night. Once that had been the norm, but now, she couldn't even imagine the man she loved coming home to her bed. No. That wouldn't work. Not yet.

~

CURTIS KNOCKED ON THE DOOR AT SEVEN O'CLOCK SHARP. HE'D never found the need to change his clothes several times before taking a woman out, but this was different. This was Simone.

At first he'd been excited at the opportunity to spend the evening with her. He'd showered, shaved, and dressed in his best *going out* jeans. Then he'd remembered his time with Simone.

They been so comfortable wrapped in each other's arms. He'd fallen short of telling her he loved her and he often wondered if it would have made a difference. Probably not. Women like Simone were told that too often. She probably didn't know what the words really meant. That had caused him to change into casual clothes, sweats, and back into his *going out* jeans.

An anxious buzz zipped through him. What was he doing? This wasn't going to end well. Oh, Simone Pierpont shows up in Nashville and claims she's going to be independent and on her own. She gives a beaten woman some earrings and begs her best friend for a job. Was that really that heroic?

Curtis stepped down one of the front steps, and then another. This was silly. She was going to run him over the coals again, and he'd be the fool.

He was almost all the way down the steps when Simone finally opened the door. Her hair hung in a low pony tail over her shoulder. She was dressed in his sister's clothes and she looked absolutely adorable.

The active male in him said to scoop her off her feet, throw her onto that waterbed, and forget the rest of the world.

But the logical man said to smile and keep his distance the rest of the night.

Somewhere in between those two, Curtis made it back up the stairs and decided to forget the rest of the world, but to keep his distance at the same time.

CYNTHIA HAD SAID TO MEET THEM DOWNTOWN, BUT BY CURTIS' estimations she'd started her own party hours earlier. The moment they walked into the club, she ran to them, draped her arms over each of them, and slurred her adoration for them both.

"C'mon. C'mon. Let's drink." She pulled them to her table where Sam already sat.

She fell down in the seat next to Sam. He put his arm around her and held her upright in the chair.

Curtis shook his head. Sadly, he saw many of his coworkers in this same light too often. This was how they forgot the stresses of their jobs.

"I'll get us some drinks. Do you want a beer or a glass of wine," he asked Simone.

"I would like an iced tea."

He focused on her. "Iced tea."

"Yes. Is that a problem?"

"Not usually. We're out to let go of the week. You can't do that on iced tea."

She smiled, but it wasn't a happy smile. It was one he'd seen her use before. It was her smile that gave her power over anyone who challenged her. "I think I will be happy with the tea."

He nodded and headed toward the bar.

Curtis placed his orders and turned to find Sam walking toward him. "How long has she been at it?" He nodded toward Cynthia.

"She was already toasted when I picked her up"

"What's that about?"

Sam shrugged. "She's just unwinding."

"You're getting her another?"

"O'Douls." He laughed. "At this point she'll never know."

Sam was good people, Curtis knew that. He could rest assured that Simone would be in good hands living with Sam.

CHAPTER 22

*S*imone was well into her second iced tea when she thought she might explode. Sam and Cynthia had danced for nearly an hour, but she'd stayed at the table and Curtis had never left her side.

"I have to use the ladies room," she hollered over the music.

"C'mon, I'll walk you. It's across over there." He pointed to the back of the establishment.

"I'll be fine." She stood from her stool.

Curtis took hold of her hand. "I don't trust a single one of those cowboys. You're mine for the night, and I'm going to keep it that way."

The statement was just that, a statement, and if she read too much into it she knew she'd be setting herself up for disappointment.

Because she had no choice, and she had to get to the bathroom, she let him hold tight to her hand as they walked through the crowd. His words still rang in her ears. Did he not trust the cowboys or did he not trust her? She didn't like the way he'd put it to her. Did he still see her as someone who would ditch him there and go home with someone else? Well, he must have or he wouldn't have said such a thing. Then again, why wouldn't he think that?

When she walked out of the restroom, he was standing there, leaned against the wall waiting for her. His booted feet crossed at the ankles and his thumbs hooked through his belt loops made him lengthy and sexy. She couldn't imagine there was another *cowboy* in that bar that could turn her head as the doctor with the deep blue eyes had.

"C'mon." He took hold of her hand. "You owe me a dance."

"I cannot dance." Her voice shook as much as her hands.

"You can, but let me teach you how we do it in Tennessee."

He pulled her to the dance floor and slid his arm around her waist. Her entire body quivered as his hand settled against the small of her back. This was how it had all started. The hand, the gaze, her body pressed to his—the kiss which had followed.

She tilted her head and their eyes locked. He'd felt it too, she was certain.

People moved around them, but they stood there gazing at one another. His Adam's apple bobbed in his throat. Was it true she could make him feel as overwhelmed as she felt?

Curtis pulled her closer. The anticipation of him kissing her was overpowering. She braced herself. If their lips met the entire earth would move.

Instead, he took hold of her right hand. "Follow my lead. Quick. Quick. Slow. Slow."

"What?" Her voice was airy, but the sound around them hushed her tone.

"Follow my lead. I'm teaching you to dance."

Simone mimicked his moves. She'd been trained to dance with a partner, so following him shouldn't have been a problem. Her only problem was she'd been taught to dance on the balls of her feet. The boots she'd worn inhibited her drastically.

Laugher swelled in her chest as she quickly moved against him with her right foot and stepped on him. "I am sorry."

"Happens all the time. Quick. Quick. Slow. Slow." He continued to repeat the steps until she had mastered them. Once she had, he began to move her in circles with the same footwork.

They'd successfully moved around the dance floor without falling. He'd moved her in circles, and now he spun her as the song ended, and pulled her in tight and close to him. She could feel his heart beat against her chest and she knew it was more than the dancing.

The music changed, the rhythm slowed, and Curtis' arm wrapped around her tighter.

He let go of her right hand and cupped the back of her neck. Instinctively she placed her hands on his chest as they rocked back and forth to the music.

They'd danced this way at Carlos' wedding. It was then he'd kissed her the first time. It was her own fault, before the night was over they were naked behind the barn. It wouldn't end that way tonight, but as she took a breath to speak and explain that they should leave, he moved in, tipping his head and brushing her lips with his.

Any logical thought she'd had slipped away as his warm and pliant mouth worked against hers.

She wasn't sure if they were still moving or if it was her head swimming in the moment. Could she possibly hold him in that place forever? If only he'd want her like this forever, everything she'd ever done, and the secrets she held, wouldn't be a problem.

His fingers massaged the back of her neck as his tongue sought hers, the music still surrounding them.

Simone's fingers gripped the front of his shirt as he took the kiss even deeper on the dance floor.

The world moved around them and she lost herself in the memory of what they'd had, alone, in his apartment and on the yacht. Why had she been so foolish to walk away from all of that?

Curtis pulled back and rested his forehead against hers. "I'm sorry. I got carried away having you this close." He moved until they were dancing with the other couples on the floor.

"I did not mind."

He swallowed hard. "I'd like to continue that."

"Curtis…"

"Simone, don't turn me away again."

He spun her around the floor until they were off to the side and he turned her until her back pushed up against the wall. His mouth was quick and hot on hers again, and everything, everyone, disappeared.

Her heart pounded in her ears as loud as the music. Her breath was hard to recover.

When he pulled his lips from hers it was all she could do not to grab him and pull him back into her secluded world in her head.

His breath was quick too and there was a fog over his eyes telling her he was in as deep as she was. Things were stirring in both of them.

"Tell me why," he whispered heavily in her ear.

"Why? Why what?" She was breathless from his cologne which carried on the air, the spinning dance, the kiss that made her mindless.

He placed a kiss on her neck and she could feel her own pulse jut up under his lips. "Why did you leave me?"

Her eyes closed and her breath caught in her chest. "Oh, Curtis, please…"

"If I meant nothing you wouldn't be here now, right?" He kissed the other side of her neck just below her ear lobe.

She was pinned there, there was no escape, and she was sure that had been the plan.

Curtis nuzzled his face next to hers and her mind was cluttering with everything she wanted to say. "You meant everything to me," she said breathless and on the brink of spilling her secret.

He rested his forehead against hers again. "Is that why you're here? Is that why you came to Nashville?"

This wasn't where she wanted to have this conversation, but there didn't seem to be much choice. "I know you will never forgive me for what I did. But yes. I came here because I knew Zach would help me, and I knew that you would be here no matter what."

"We can start over, Simone." His hands moved up and into her hair. His body pressed even harder to hers. "Pretend like the yacht never happened." He brushed her lips with his. "Let me take you home." He nipped her lips with a kiss. "Let me stay." He pushed closer to her and she could feel the heat from his body penetrate through her clothing.

"Curtis." She said it without the airy, sexy appeal and he stepped back. "I want this. And you are right, I want to start over again."

"Good." He moved in and kissed her neck again.

She pushed him back. "When you take me home, you have to leave. Let's do this right, okay? I don't want to mess it up again."

CHAPTER 23

*S*imone had pulled Curtis in for one more kiss, right there on that dance floor. What her words said and what her body had said were two different things. But as he drove her home, her head rested on his shoulder, her fingers intertwined with his, he knew he could do this.

For heaven's sake, he was a man well into his thirties. He'd spent the night with enough women he knew how it worked. Likewise, he'd been turned down enough too. This was nothing new—but this was Simone.

Oh, Simone. Her French accent filled his ears even when she wasn't near him. Her fragrance tantalized his senses even when it didn't carry on the breeze. Her hair, nearly black, curtained him as she lay atop him, staring down at him with those deep blue eyes; the memory of it kept him awake at nights. She'd crept into his subconscious and that had been very dangerous.

It affected his work, his friendships, and his relationship with his family. There had been a few weeks when he hadn't even spoken to his sister or her husband because of Simone. That wasn't right. No woman should come between family. But it had.

Simone quickly sat up from her position next to him. "Curtis, pull over."

"What?"

"Pull over." She was frantic.

"You're not leaving me from a moving vehicle." He'd be damned if she was going to do this to him again. What had he been thinking? Why had he bothered? Why...

"I am going to be sick."

Curtis pulled to the side of the road and Simone jumped out of the truck. She made for the first bank of trees and before he could get to her she'd gotten sick.

"Sweetheart, are you okay?"

"Go away." She wouldn't turn toward him. "Let me be for a moment."

"I'm a doctor. I've seen people get sick."

She held her hand up to ward him off. "Not me. Now go away."

He took a few steps back toward the truck before she threw up again. When she was done, she stood there for a moment. She reached into her purse, which hung from her shoulder, and pulled out a tissue. She wiped her face and then ran her fingers under her eyes. When she was composed, she turned back to him.

"I am very sorry," her voice shook and she kept her eyes diverted to the ground.

"It's really not a problem. Are you okay?"

"I'm fine." She walked past him and climbed back in the truck.

Curtis followed and stood at the door. "I told Zach I didn't think you were feeling well."

With that she tensed in the seat. "Doctor Keller, I am fine. It has been a busy week. I have not been eating as I am accustomed to. Please just take me home."

"I'll take you home, and then I'm staying." He shut the door and walked around the truck. By the time he'd climbed in behind the steering wheels Simone was sobbing. "Sweetheart, what is wrong?"

"I left you on that yacht." She sucked up a breath. "I should not have done that."

"No, you shouldn't have. But I made it home." He put the truck in drive. "It took me six days, but I made it."

There was a slight chuckle that came from the sobbing mess of a woman next to him, but then the tears started all over again.

"Curtis, first, you cannot stay. Those are my rules. Second," she took another deep breath and paused, causing him to turn his head toward her. "I left you on that yacht because I did not know what to do. I had never been in love with anyone before."

Thank God for the stoplight. Curtis jerked the truck as he stopped and turned to her. "Love?" His voice cracked and that alone told him to stop the conversation and steer it in another direction.

"I know, it sounds silly, really. But yes." She finally turned to him. Her makeup had smeared, her eyes were bloodshot, and her hair matted to her face. She was beautiful.

"I fell in love with you, Curtis, and it scared me to death."

He'd like to laugh at her, but he couldn't. In fact, he understood her completely.

The light turned green and Curtis eased off the break. For a moment, he had nothing to say, and he knew that was eating her up by the way she tore the tissue in her hand into tiny pieces.

"Simone, I understand."

"You do? How could you? It is quite silly."

"I understand, because if anyone else had left me stranded in the ocean, I wouldn't be trying so desperately to spend time with them, no matter how crazy they made me."

"Curtis, what are you saying?"

He glanced at her and then turned his attention back to the road. "I'm saying, that I felt the same way." He pulled up to her apartment building, parked the truck, and then turned toward her. "At first I was worried sick about you. I thought maybe you'd fallen overboard and I'd lost you."

She covered her mouth and the tears were back. "I did not know that. I did not think of that."

"I spent two hours trying to figure out what might have happened and yelling for you, as if you'd appear out of the water. I couldn't quite figure out the radio, but eventually I got it and called for help. I told them I'd lost you overboard."

"Oh, Curtis."

"Someone knew where you were because when they got to me, and I was frantic, they told me you'd been taken to the mainland on a private boat."

"I am so sorry."

"I'd never been so scared, and that should say a lot since I work in an E.R. and I've seen my sister lying there beaten and undergoing a C-section. But the difference was, I was there and I could help her. I didn't know where you were and I couldn't help you."

The sobs were stronger now and he hated that he was causing them, but she needed to know what went on while she gallivanted off into her private life.

She wiped at the tears that kept forming. "How can you even be this close to me? I was horrible."

"For the same reason you left."

Her head shot up and her eyes opened wide.

Curtis reached out his hand and caressed her wet cheek. "I fell in love with you, Simone."

Her jaw trembled and a line of worry creased her forehead. "You did?"

He nodded. "I did."

She looked down at her hands. "What an idiot I was."

"You were scared."

"I am still scared."

"But you're here." He let his hand drop and gathered hers in his. "I'm not going anywhere. I'm here and now so are you. We can try again."

"You really care about me that much, after what I did?"

He took a deep breath and made sure his mind was clear. What he was about to say wasn't anything he'd said to anyone else before. "Simone, I forgive you."

NOT MANY PEOPLE SURPRISED SIMONE PIERPONT, EXCEPT HER father when he'd banished her from his office, and now Curtis Keller.

She'd been taught to remain in control no matter the situation, but what was she supposed to do when everything fell into place?

Her throat went dry and the pace of her heart ramped up. "You forgive me?"

"I can't say I'm not pissed that it had to come about this way. But I forgive you for leaving me."

"Oh, Curtis." Why couldn't she control her tears?

He scooped her up in his arms and held her against his chest. "I didn't think you were this girly," he chuckled and then kissed the top of her head.

"I want this to work. I really want this to work."

"Then we have to work at it."

She nodded and sat back to wipe her eyes.

"Now," he brushed her cheek with this thumb, "are you going to let me stay the night to make sure you're okay?"

Through her tears she shook her head. "No. I am fine, and I want our next time to be special."

"You're killing me."

"I know." She took his hands in hers and held them tight. "Let me make dinner for you tomorrow."

"You cook?"

She didn't appreciate the tone in his voice. But then he

couldn't have expected anything else. And no, she didn't know how to cook, but she'd figure something out. She'd do anything to impress him. Cooking for him might have the opposite effect, but she'd call for reinforcements if she had to.

Simone lifted his fingers to her lips. "I will make dinner for you tomorrow. And I will make it very special."

"I suppose I'm man enough to wait one more day. But I'm also man enough to still ask one more time, can I come in?"

She smiled as she eased her hand toward the door handle. "Tomorrow. Seven o'clock. Dinner."

"I'll be here."

Simone opened the door and eased out of the seat just as Curtis opened his door. "No. I know you are a gentleman, and my father would kill us both if you did not walk me to the door, but I am asking you to stay." He eased back in his seat and her heart began to ease its pace. "Goodnight, Curtis."

"Good night, Simone."

She shut the door and hurried up the stairs, her mind already flooded with the night she'd plan for him tomorrow. He was right where she needed him. Forgiveness had been passed to her, the word love flowed between both of them, and kisses had been had. There would be no turning her away when she told him about the baby. By tomorrow night, Simone would have everything she never knew she'd wanted.

CHAPTER 24

*C*urtis didn't sleep as soundly as he'd hoped he would. Thoughts of his arms wrapped around Simone at the club had his mind drifting further back to them making love under the star filled sky, alone, on the yacht. He also considered that his mind was completely lost and giving Simone a second chance to break his heart was just asking for her to do so.

And yet, still, there was the whole fact that Simone had moved to the states, landed a data entry job of all things, and now lived with a man she'd only met—something had happened in her quaint little life and before he had dinner with her he'd head to Zach's and see what he'd found out.

Later that morning, when he pulled up in front of his sister's house, he noticed the familiar extra car that was always kept in their garage. His sister Arianna must be in town, as that was her ride when she'd come back home.

Before he even reached the front door, he heard the distinct laughter he'd grown up with and found he missed dearly. It came from the back of the house. He walked around back and there sat his sisters, still lounging in their pajamas on the back porch drinking coffee.

"I hope that's decaf," he called out as Regan took a sip from her mug.

She turned to see him walking toward them. "You worry too much, and if you must know, yes, it's decaf."

Arianna stood from her seat and started down the back steps of the porch to meet him. She wrapped her arms around him and planted a noisy kiss on his cheek. "I miss you, criss-cross-eyes."

He chuckled at the childhood name she would still call him in the confines of family. "I miss you too blueberry-head." He reached up and mussed up her already tussled hair. "Why did you always call me that?"

"It pissed you off."

"As an adult I completely understand the logic in that."

He followed her up the steps and took the vacant chair next to her.

Regan was examining him. He could feel her eyes on him long before he looked up at her. She pursed her lips and narrowed her eyes. "Something is up with you."

"Usually."

"You and Simone worked things out didn't you?"

Curtis laughed, reached over, and took her mug of coffee out of her hand. He took a sip and handed it back. "Why do you put that crap in your coffee?"

"Cheaper than Starbucks."

"Hmmm, I suppose."

Arianna nudged him in the arm. "Stop skirting the question. Did you mend things up with the princess?"

He nudged his sister back and looked at Regan. "You didn't tell her?"

"She got here at midnight, and here you are interrupting my gossip session. How was I supposed to tell her?"

Curtis laughed at his sister who did enjoy gossiping with her sister and their sister-in-law Madeline, but who wouldn't take gossip out on the street. It wasn't her style.

He leaned back in his seat and looked at Arianna, who with her hair piled atop her head, makeup traces still lingering around her eyes, and a new tattoo on her ankle, looked content in her own skin as always.

"Simone moved to Nashville a few weeks ago. She decided to shuck the life of an oil heiress, get a job, wear hand-me-downs, and live in a little apartment with a male nurse from the clinic she works in."

Arianna's eyes opened wide. "Simone is working—in a clinic?"

"Yep. Cynthia, of all people, got her the job."

Arianna lifted her mug to her lips. "Cynthia. That's your safe date right?"

He noticed Regan reached for her cup quickly and lifted it to her mouth to hide her grin.

"Yeah, real safe," he said with a shake of his head.

Arianna kicked him with a quick swing of her bare foot. "You still didn't answer our question. Did you mend things with her?"

He gave some thought to what he wanted to say. There was no reason to get their tongues wagging, but they knew him too well and no matter what he said, they'd see through it. "We have an understanding. We're going to work at a relationship while she's here."

Regan sat up in her seat. "While she's here? Is she already planning on leaving?"

"No, she seems content. But c'mon. She's going to give up a lifetime of glamour and glitz to live here?"

"Why would she do this if she planned to go back?" Arianna asked.

Curtis shrugged. "I just don't think this is forever. She got scared because we felt things neither of us felt before and she ran off."

"And you're okay with that?"

"No." It was matter-of-fact enough, and he was sure he

believed it, but his stomach did a little uncomfortable squeeze when he thought about it. "I've never felt this for anyone else."

"Felt what?" Arianna's eyes narrowed in that *give-me-an-answer* look. She was fishing for what she wanted to hear. Yep, this was how his sisters rolled.

"Fine. I think I'm in love with her."

Both of his sisters giggled and moved in to smother him with hugs and kisses. He'd known better, he really had.

"You'll run him off with that," Zach said standing at the door.

Arianna sat back. "Eh, wouldn't be the first time."

"Hey, Curtis. Why don't you come in and have some real coffee."

"It's got to be a better offer than sitting here drinking this frilly stuff and getting mauled." He stood and followed Zach into the house.

Zach walked to the counter where a fresh pot of coffee finished brewing. He took down two mugs. "I talked to Simone's father the other day."

"Oh, yeah? He wonder when she's headed back too?"

Zach slid him a look of concern then focused back on the coffee maker. "You sound like you doubt her reasoning for staying."

"What I doubt is that someone can change so quickly. I mean why give it all up to move here and work in some menial hourly job?"

Zach picked up the pot of coffee and filled each mug before setting the pot back in the maker. He handed a mug to Curtis. "You don't think someone can change?"

"Well sure they can, but…"

"But why do it?"

"Right?"

"Maybe she just wants to be near you."

Curtis followed Zach to the table and each of them sat down. Curtis sipped his coffee and then set it down in front of him. His hands were trembling and that wasn't a good sign. It meant she'd gotten under his skin and he'd lost more sleep than he'd thought he had.

"Simone and I have come to an agreement to work on things." He let out a breath. "I think I love her, man, and I don't want to."

Zach smiled as he leaned back in his seat. "I knew you did. And likewise I've never seen her as crazy over a man before."

"Yeah, and I know she's had plenty." That sounded rude and he hadn't meant to be, he was just trying to justify his uncertainty.

Zach must have known he'd regretted what he'd said because he didn't call him on it or his own mishandlings with women. "You're going to give a relationship a try then?"

"Yeah. I guess we are." He chuckled. "She must be pretty serious about doing it right too. She wouldn't even let me stay last night, even after she got sick."

"Sick?" Zach inched forward. "Is she okay?"

"I think her nerves got the better of her. She's fine. She's cooking me dinner tonight."

That made Zach laugh aloud. "Simone? Cook? She really must be sick."

"Well that's what I thought, but if she's into changing everything I guess she'll cook too."

"She must have it bad for you."

Though he thought he was a catch, he didn't see giving up her livelihood for him. That still didn't make sense.

Curtis lifted his mug. "Anyway, you said you talked to her father?"

"I did. I don't think she'd want me to tell you what he said though."

He let the hot coffee sear his throat. "So why bring it up?"

"Because I now know you love her and you'll want to do what is right for her."

Curtis' hands tensed around his mug. Well there ya go. Now it was his job to take care of the righteous princess who decided she was now common folk. "So why is she here?"

"He cut her off."

Curtis waited a moment for more, but Zach said nothing. "That's it? He cut her off? What did she buy one too many pairs of Italian shoes?"

Zach shook his head and leaned over the table. "I think there is more to it than that. He didn't want to talk about her. As far as he was concerned he had no daughter. And he threatened to not do business with me if I mentioned her again."

Curtis eased back in his chair. "That seems serious."

"I think it is. I don't know what she did, and she wouldn't tell me. But maybe she'll tell you."

He seriously doubted that, but now he had a mission. Why was his Parisian beauty taking the low life?

CHAPTER 25

*W*hat had she been thinking? She wasn't sure she could boil water in a pot let alone a full meal. This was it. She was going to fail miserably.

She'd walked around the grocery store for a half hour, searching, hopelessly for any idea. She'd left with only a bottle of nail polish remover and a nail file to fix her chipped manicure. It might be a long while before she could have the luxury of a manicure again. But she was at a total loss as to what to prepare for Curtis for dinner.

Unless—she knew it was the right idea—she begged Regan for her help.

Simone called Zach for his wife's phone number. She'd wished she'd have memorized her number too, but she'd called Zach so many times over the years it was quite literally the only phone number she'd known without her cell phone, which she'd had to relinquish.

Two hours after finally tracking her down, Regan was standing at Simone's front door with a bag full of groceries and a grin on her lips that told Simone she was going to owe her big for this.

"If you're going to impress him make chicken piccata." She set the bags on the counter and then with her hands on the small of her back stretched.

Panic had already set in, but Simon's hands shook as she opened the first bag. "I cannot make anything. I do not know why I told him to come."

"Because a smitten woman will do stupid things to make the man she's crazy for spend some time with her."

"Is that what I am? Smitten?"

"Oh, honey, I think you're fully in love, but I'll leave it at smitten and let you two decide." She pulled the package of chicken from another bag and then a box of noodles. "Now we need a pot and a pan."

Simone bit down on her lip and looked around the kitchen. She opened the cupboard under the stove. At least she had some domestic intuition.

She set the pot and pan on the stove and began taking any instruction Regan gave to her as they began to build a dinner to impress the man she did love. After all, tonight was big. She needed him to maintain his forgiveness and dwell on the fact he'd fallen in love with her. She needed him to be ecstatic over the news when she told him she was carrying his baby. There was no other option, and when her mind drifted to any negative thoughts about it she made herself think about how happy they could be together.

Simone watched Regan move about the kitchen as if it were her own. How did a woman do it—raise a baby, keep a husband happy, and wear a smile as she turned chicken in a pan with a pair of tongs? Her own mother had been miserable with diamonds, shoes, and a beach front back yard where the yacht was parked for her convenience in any one of their homes. Sure, Regan was a pampered wife, but no matter how wealthy Zachary Benson was, there was more to her wealth. He loved his wife and his child. He loved them both enough to want to have more children—that was the kind of wealth Simone had always longed for.

Even as children, Zach's relationship with his parents was unique to her. Sure, they'd tucked him away in a French boarding school, but it was for his betterment. For her, they just wanted her tucked away. There were mistresses to have. Parties to throw. Companies to build. Children were in the way for the Pierponts.

"You look lost."

Regan's voice caught her off guard.

"I guess my mind was a million miles away."

"Happens to me all the time," she said as she pulled the chicken from the pan and set it to the side. "Especially now that I'm pregnant, I feel as though I can't keep a simple thought in my mind."

Her curiosity had peaked. She needed to tread lightly, but she had her own questions about what was going on within her body. What better a time to ask, but she had to be careful.

"So how do you mean you cannot keep a thought?"

"Pregnant brain. Theory is there is too much blood going to your stomach not enough in your head, or something like that. You just forget things. I did it with Tyler all the time."

"Really?"

"Sure. But now mix that with just being tired, because I have a toddler who wants to play every morning at two o'clock. I think it's worse this time."

Simone moved to the refrigerator and took out the bag of pre-washed salad Regan had brought. She searched for a bowl and dumped it inside and then set it on the table.

"Do you think this will be your last baby?" Simone asked as casually as she could.

"No." Regan's answer was quick and firm. "I want two more."

"Really?"

Regan turned and smiled at her. "You seem surprised."

"Do I? It just seems like a lot of work."

"You can guarantee it." Regan opened the bottle of white wine she'd brought and poured it into the pan with the drippings from the chicken. "I grew up in a noisy, chaotic house. I want that for Tyler. I want him to have what I still have with Arianna, Curtis, and Carlos."

Simone wanted that too, not only for her baby, but for herself. She'd never had brothers or sisters. Zach was as close as they came. But she had a unique opportunity now. If things worked out with Curtis she'd have sisters. She'd have brothers. She'd be part of a family. Already they'd accepted her and she was an outsider.

Tears welled in her eyes, but she wasn't quick enough to brush them away before they fell.

Regan placed the spaghetti noodles in the pot of boiling water and looked over at her. "Why are you crying?"

"I am a bit overwhelmed lately. That is all." Simone brushed away her tears. "I have never had what you had. Money cannot buy the fond memories you have with your family. Your family rallied behind you when you met Zach and when Madeline was sick you all were there to support her even when she was not married to your brother. I know for a fact you have never missed one show Arianna has had on Broadway. And here you are cooking for me. I have never had such an experience as compassion in my life."

Regan studied her for a moment. "Why are you here, Simone? Why now?"

"My father does not want me. I have dishonored him."

"No matter what you've done, a father will forgive you."

She shook her head. "Mine would rather dangle my trust fund over my head and threaten me. I think I surprised him when I told him I would rather live on my own than be bribed with his wealth all the time."

"That's a pretty big statement right there."

"It was a pretty big decision." She searched for two glasses in the cupboard and set them on the table. "You have money now. Do you think you are happier?"

Regan laughed. "I'm happier because I have Zach. But I had days when all I could afford was packaged noodles, and I was happy."

That confirmed what Cynthia had told her. "Why?"

"Because I was doing what I wanted to do." Regan smiled as she lifted the noodles from the pot and placed them in the bowl. "I lived in L.A. in a tiny little apartment I shared with another girl I didn't know well. Kind of like you and Sam. But I was broke. I could afford my car, my share of the rent, and a few groceries. And aside from my wonderful life now, I don't think you could top the feeling of freedom I had."

Oddly enough, Simone understood that. Lunch at her desk, the very first day she worked at the clinic, which she'd purchased from the vending machines, had been nearly as freeing as walking away from her father when he'd told her to get rid of the baby or lose everything she had. He'd been worried about her disgracing his name. She was a fully grown, mature adult, and yet he could still make her feel like a child. But sitting in the small, rundown kitchen of the small shared apartment, she didn't feel like a child. She finally felt hope spurring through her. Her father was small minded. There was a whole new world at her feet. She just had to keep her feet firmly planted.

"Oh, dear it is six-fifty. I need to disappear." Regan began to scurry about finishing up the small parts of the dinner she'd created while Simone did the small parts that hadn't involved the stove. "Plate the chicken on top of the noodles and drizzle the caper sauce over that."

She reached for her purse and pulled out her keys.

"I stuck a cheesecake in the fridge for after, too," she said smiling as she hurried for the door.

"Thank you from the bottom of my heart."

"This is what sisters do." She kissed Simone on the cheek and hurried down the front steps.

Simone shut the door and rested against it. *Sisters.* That was a hefty word.

She stood there a moment longer and let her nerves settle. Everything had to go right. She wanted Curtis to be hers more now that she had before. He had more to offer a relationship than just himself. He had a family and Simone was desperately in need of a family.

CHAPTER 26

$\mathcal{C}$urtis peered through the small window next to the door and watched as Simone moved through the apartment fluffing pillows and lighting candles. He was sure that was as domestic as she got, but it would be fun to see if she fessed up to her dinner preparation.

He stepped back and knocked.

Simone opened the door. Her hair fell like black satin over her shoulders and she looked nearly virginal in her white cotton shirt, belted at the waist over a pair of white pants. Her hair and the white of her outfit were fitting for the contrast going through him. Hot and cold. Good and bad. Love and hate.

"You look beautiful," he finally said after realizing he'd stood there long enough just staring at her.

"Thank you." She stepped back. "Come in."

Curtis stepped through the door and their bodies brushed. He felt her suck in a breath and he'd quickly considered scooping her up and laying her down on the couch. Forget dinner, but that wasn't what she wanted and he knew it.

He sniffed the fragrant air. "Chicken piccata?"

"I was told it was your favorite."

He smiled. There was no keeping any secrets from her. "I saw Regan turn the corner when I pulled up."

Simone's shoulders dropped and a crease formed in her forehead. "I did not know what else to do."

Curtis gathered her in his arms and gazed down into her blue eyes. "I think it was sweet you asked her to help you."

"Help? She did it all. I was lost in the store and the kitchen. I am a wreck."

He wanted to laugh at her, but he couldn't. She was sincere and totally defenseless for the first time. "You're wonderful."

The crease eased between her brows and a smile formed on her lips. "I wanted to impress you."

"You did that a long time ago." He brushed his fingers through her hair. "But considering it is cooked and ready to eat, I suppose kissing you senseless will have to wait."

"Well," she inched up closer to him, "a few kisses wouldn't hurt."

That was all he needed to hear. He hoisted her to his hips and her legs wrapped around him. This was familiar. This was comfort when it came to Simone.

He pressed her back up against the wall and drove himself mad with the kiss he planted on her.

Her fingers tangled in his hair. Her legs tightened around him for support. And her breasts pressed against his chest and heaved from the breath she fought for.

When he couldn't stand there any longer without carrying her away he set her down and eased back the kiss.

"I am glad we did not make appetizers. I think that was appetizer enough."

"Yep." It didn't sound intelligent, but it was all he could get out as he tried to will his body to ease.

. . .

SIMONE LED HIM TO THE SMALL KITCHEN WHERE SHE'D SET A proper table with mismatched plates and silverware.

"I saw a beer in the refrigerator if you would like one."

"Thanks, but I'm on call."

"Oh," she said trying to hide the disappointment in her voice as she reached for the serving platter. "I did not realize that."

"I forgot. I was too busy kissing you." He reached for her and his fingers brushed down her arm.

Her chest fluttered knowing he was there with her, wanting to kiss her, talking sweetly to her. Perhaps it was the perfect opportunity to just tell him about the baby.

Gathering her courage, she took a deep cleansing breath. "I am glad you came tonight. I have dreamed about this for months."

She took her seat as he began to serve them both from the platter she'd set on the table. "You thought about cooking me dinner?"

Simone could feel the heat rise in her cheeks. "Curtis," he looked up at her. "Since I left you I have thought of you every day. And after having spent the afternoon with your sister I realized that there were so many wonderful things you brought to my life, and not just physically."

Curtis sat back in his chair. "I don't think I understand."

"This is very difficult for me." She took her paper napkin out from beneath her fork and set it in her lap. "I see what you have with your siblings and I realize I missed out on that."

He narrowed his eyes. "So you love me for my family?"

"And your charming smile." She joked.

"I am very dashing."

She laughed and he placed salad on her plate.

"What I am very badly trying to say is that I want to be part of your family. I want to have a family like yours."

Curtis leaned back in his seat again, draping his arm over the back. He watched her for a moment. "This sounds like a marriage proposal, but I'm not sure it is me you want to marry. I think you'd rather marry my family."

She swallowed hard. Why couldn't she just get it out? "Oh, you would think I could say this without messing it up. After all, I was trained my whole life to help sell big deals."

"Now you're selling me something?"

"Me," she said simply.

He eased forward. "I am sold on you."

She let out the breath that had stuck in her lungs. "Good. Then..."

Her thought was interrupted by his pager going off on his waist and only a moment later his cell phone rang from his pocket.

"Are you kidding me?" He silenced the pager and looked at the display on the phone before answering. "Dr. Keller—yes, how many? The clinic? The E.R.?" He let out loud breath. "Fifteen minutes away."

Simone sat silent at the table as she listened to him ramble off miscellaneous words. Before he disconnected the call, he was already standing, his truck keys pulled out of his pocket.

He looked down at her seated at the table. "Simone, I'm so sorry. There was a carbon monoxide leak at some club. The hospital is flooded. I have to go."

It was that very moment she understood what Cynthia had said about not wanting to marry Dr. Curtis Keller. He was already married to his job. If he were her husband, this would be the norm. He'd jump up from dinner and race out the door. What would happen if their son was pitching baseball game or their daughter was in the middle of a dance recital?

"Simone, I'm sorry." He headed for the door and she quickly followed. "Listen, I have no idea what time I'll get out of there. Or if I'll get out of there." He leaned in and kissed her cheek. "If I can, I'll try to stop back by, but..." He was already out the door and hurrying down the steps to his truck. Only a moment later he was gone.

She watched him speed away before shutting the door and walking back into the kitchen. There sat the meal Regan had prepared—untouched.

The tears started from the pit of her stomach and burned her chest as they made their way to her eyes. Why did she even think a man like Curtis Keller would want to love someone? He was married to his job and his patients. Only someone like Cynthia who was immersed into that kind of life would understand him. He was good only for quick romps behind barns, a friend with benefits. Curtis Keller wasn't the father type. He might be compassionate and caring, but not for the people who really mattered—the woman who loved him and the baby who would want to love him too.

Simone sat at the table and pushed the plate in front of her away. Why did she think she could do this? Why did she come all the way to America only to find out she should have stayed in Paris? Eventually she could have convinced her father he was wrong. Whatever it was that had driven her to Nashville had been a mistake. It was time to realize that it was a lost cause to think that Curtis would choose her.

CHAPTER 27

*I*t had taken everything within Simone's power to not throw dinner in the trash. She was mad and normally that meant making a scene. But wasn't that why she was in Nashville in the first place? In a battle of words with her father, she'd lost her temper, lost everything she'd ever know, and now sat alone in a horrible little apartment feeling sorry for herself.

She searched the kitchen for storage containers and packaged up the dinner. If Curtis did show up, she'd feed him. She'd tell him about the baby, and then decide how she'd make plans to head back to the life she knew.

"It smells good in here." Sam stood in the doorway of the kitchen. "Got any left over?"

Simone let out a breath and smiled at him. "Of course. Sit down."

Sam washed his hands and Simone made him a plate of food as he sat down at the table.

"Did you eat all ready?"

She sat down across from him and watched as he cut into the chicken on his plate. "I was trying to impress Curtis."

"He got called out on the carbon monoxide call, didn't he?"

She nodded.

"The clinic was packed." He took a bite. "This is great. You make this?"

"Regan." She watched him take another bite. "If the clinic was full, why are you home?"

"Shift was over," he said with his mouth full.

And just like that she knew her fate was sealed. She'd personally seen Sam work with his patients and he had just as much compassion as Curtis, but Curtis would always run out and back to the job he was married to—Sam would go home to his family.

"So," he stood to retrieve the beer from the refrigerator, "what are you doing with the rest of your night?"

Simone shrugged. "Nothing I guess."

"Star Wars marathon is on TV. Want to pop some popcorn and watch?"

Sam was easy to get along with and she was comfortable with him. Never in her life had she sat on a couch and watched a marathon of movies with popcorn. Suddenly her ruined evening didn't seem so bad.

"Regan brought a cheesecake. We could just go in after it with two forks."

Sam took a pull of his beer and then laughed. "That's my girl. Go get something on that's comfy. You look too uptight."

He dumped his plate in the sink and headed out to the couch.

Simone looked down at her outfit. It was very obvious that she was out of place in Nashville. Even in her own home she was dressed as though she were on parade.

She'd found a pair of pajama shorts in the clothes Regan had given her and a loose T-shirt. She knotted her hair on the top of her head and had taken a moment to wash off her makeup.

Sam was already sitting on the couch, his feet up on the coffee table, when Simone emerged from her bedroom. Star Wars played on the television and the cheesecake sat next to him with a fork stuck in the middle.

He looked up at her when he heard her. "Couldn't help myself. I started it."

Sam patted the seat on the couch next to him. He moved the cheesecake to the coffee table and Simone took the seat he offered.

"Have you seen these movies?"

She sat stiff and upright next to him. "Of course."

"Cool. Sit back and relax. Kick your feet up." He tucked his arm under her legs and lifted them up. "You need to relax."

Simone sat back and tried to loosen up. Old habits were hard to break.

Sam picked up the cheesecake, handed her a fork, and began digging into the center of the cake.

Simone took a small bite.

"You have to dig in. You can't just take little bites."

She laughed. "I did not know there was an art to this."

"Pigging out on the couch. Heck yeah." Sam took her fork out of her hand and dug up a big piece. He held it to her lips like a parent feeding a child. "C'mon, open up."

Simone parted her lips slightly and inched toward the fork.

Sam pulled it back. "You can't do this can you?"

"Why would I want to?"

"To be normal. Now open."

She opened her mouth a bit wider, but before she knew it he had taken another piece of the cheesecake and shoved it into her mouth like a groom would shove wedding cake into his wife's.

An evil laugh emerged from him as Simone wiped at her mouth. "Oh, God, you're a mess! This is great. How about another?"

"Are you crazy?' She wanted to laugh and cry all at the same time. What was wrong with this man she shared a home with? "Why did you do that?"

139

"Because it was funny."

"I do not see the humor," she said fighting back a laugh as she tried to scrape the smashed cheesecake off of her face.

"Oh, someday you will. You have to let go a little or you're going to go crazy when you have your baby."

$\mathcal{T}$he humor in the moment was over. Simone sat there on the beat up couch. Her face was covered in cheesecake, and she stared at Sam. Was she over reacting or did he say what she thought he had.

"I beg your pardon."

"You're almost through your first trimester, right?"

Simone swallowed hard and tears welled in her eyes. She wiped at the desert that stuck to her skin. "I never said I was pregnant."

"You didn't have to. I work with pregnant women all the time. And I have four sisters. I usually know someone is pregnant before they do."

She was finding it hard to breathe. She fought for air, but it was as if her lungs didn't know what to do with it.

Sam set down the cheesecake and placed his hands on her shoulders. "Now calm down. Don't hyperventilate on me. I've been known to be wrong in my life. So if I've said something that…"

"I am pregnant." It was only the second time she'd said it aloud to anyone and it wasn't getting any easier.

"Okay, okay. Well no need to get worked up."

"You cannot tell anyone."

He laughed and loosened his grip. "You have about three weeks before I won't have to."

"This is not a joke." She stood and rushed to the bathroom.

Sam followed her and when she looked up from the sink where she washed away his practical joke he was standing there leaning against the doorjamb, his arms crossed in front of him, and a smirk on his face.

"Curtis' baby?"

"That is none of your business."

He held his hands up in surrender. "Whatever, honey. Point is, his baby or not, if you're gonna be cooking him dinners like the one you did tonight, he'll want to know."

Simone took shallow breaths and tried to remain calm. Sam meant her no harm. Perhaps if she told someone, even Sam, she'd feel better about it.

"It happened on the yacht after Carlos' wedding to Kathy, before he married Madeline."

"Uh-huh." He nodded crossing his arms again.

"I love him. I fell in love with him in one week."

"That happens all the time."

"Not to me." She looked at herself in the mirror. At that moment she hardly recognized herself. "I left him stranded in the ocean on my father's yacht."

"Your father has a yacht?"

She snapped her head toward him. He had no idea who she was. He'd put as much faith in her as she'd put in him.

Simone nodded. "I am the heir to Pierpont Oil—or at least I was."

"No kidding." His eyes grew wide. "What the heck are you doing in Nashville then? There has to be somewhere better for you to live than here."

She shook her head. "My father cut me off from his empire when I told him I was pregnant."

"Oh."

"I have nothing."

Sam moved into the bathroom and pulled her into his arms. Her head rested below his breast bone and his enormous arms could have wrapped around her twice.

"Listen, I'm not going to tell a soul. This is for you to deal with." He stepped back, but kept his hands on her arms. "But listen, you need to be taken care of. Have you seen a doctor?"

"Once, just for confirmation."

He shook his head. "That isn't going to cut it. You need to have a checkup."

"I cannot risk Curtis or his family or Cynthia knowing yet. I am not ready."

He rubbed her arms. "Ready or not you're having a baby." He dropped his hands and took a step back. "Listen, tomorrow let's just take a look, okay? Nothing invading, we'll take our lunch in the ultrasound room and I'll look and see how the baby is doing."

Simone bit down on the inside of her cheek to force herself to keep her composure. "You would do that for me?"

"Of course."

This time she reached for him and wrapped her arms around his waist. "Thank you."

"Are you going to tell him?"

Simone stepped back and looked up at him. "I tried tonight, but he was called out."

"That's going to happen a lot."

"Cynthia said he loved his job, I just hadn't realized how much."

Sam reached up to her hair and pulled a lingering piece of cheesecake off of a loose strand. "I really don't know Curtis at all, but I know Cynthia thinks the world of him, so he must be a good person. I think he would do right by you."

"I want him to love me."

Sam laughed a hearty laugh. "I saw you two on the dance floor last night. He digs you."

"I want more than that."

He reached across to her and rested his hand on her tight stomach. "You have more than that. Give him a chance."

SIMONE CLEANED UP AGAIN HEADED BACK TO THE LIVING ROOM TO watch the movies with her very understanding roommate.

He'd cleaned up the cheesecake and was nursing another beer. She sat down next to him and kicked up her feet.

"Now you look right at home." He lifted his arm and wrapped it around her shoulders as she yawned. "You're not going to make it through all these movies, are you?"

Simone leaned into him and rested her head against his chest. "Are you?"

"Eh, I fall asleep here all the time." He reached around her with his free hand and pulled the small throw of the back of the couch. He covered her with it as she yawned again. "You know if you're far enough along we can find out the baby's sex."

She sighed. "I will think about it."

Sam kissed the top of her head and she closed her eyes. A weight had lifted from her shoulders by openly talking to Sam about the baby. Perhaps everything would be okay tomorrow. She'd let Sam do the ultrasound. And then she was most certainly going to tell Curtis.

CURTIS WAS EXHAUSTED. HE'D SEEN ALMOST ONE HUNDRED patients in the past three hours and had busted his butt to get back to Simone.

Now he stood at her front door, looking in the small window

that peered into the apartment. He wasn't sure what he'd seen unfold, but Simone had sat down on the couch in her pajamas, Sam had gathered her up in his arms, covered her with a blanket and kissed her head before she fell asleep on his chest.

His jaw hurt from gritting his teeth. Same old Simone, hopping from one man to the other, playing them all for fools. She'd stabbed him in the heart and reeled him back in again only to cozy up with the nurse. Damn he'd been stupid.

Well fire was fought with fire.

Curtis hurried down the front steps, climbed into his truck, and sped toward Cynthia's house.

CHAPTER 29

*C*ynthia wasn't happy when she pulled open the door, that much was for sure by the look in her eyes, which she'd obviously pried open from a deep sleep. But Curtis didn't care.

He quickly moved in, swept her into his arms and took possession of her mouth with his. He kicked closed the front door and a moment later had her pushed up against the wall. He'd taken her by surprise, but that was when sex with Cynthia was most fun, when it was unexpected.

Moans resonated from her throat as he skimmed his hands up and under her shirt. He pressed himself against her and that must have been what brought her from a sleep induced haze to fully awake.

Cynthia's hands came up between them and she shoved him back hard enough he stumbled.

She fixed her shirt and pushed the fallen hair out of her face. "What in the hell was that about?"

Curtis wiped his mouth with the back of his hand. When had she ever questioned his motives before?

"For the first time ever, you don't want me?" He wondered

when he'd become a cry baby, because when he said those words aloud he sounded like one.

"Want you? I was under the impression you weren't mine to take anymore."

"Meaning?"

"Meaning you and Simone were together."

He moved back toward her, but when her eyes narrowed he retreated. "Yeah, well why did I think things were going to be any different?"

"If you're going to wake me up in the middle of the night to kiss me senseless and then tell me some sob story over you and your girlfriend you're going to have to make me coffee." She headed back toward her bedroom. "I'm going to brush my teeth. Make it strong or I'll kill you."

Curtis huffed out a breath and went to make the stupid coffee. He'd come looking for sex. Just raw, going through the motion, hot, heavy, sweaty, forget any other woman existed, in the moment sex. Now he was making coffee and he knew that meant they'd be sitting at the table talking about Simone. Well he didn't want to do that. He wanted to forget all about her and absorb himself in Cynthia. It worked best that way.

He filled the coffee pot with water from the sink, taking a moment to look underneath the cupboard to make sure the pipe wasn't leaking. That looked good.

He proceeded to pour the water into the maker, missing mostly and pouring it on the counter. With a grunt, he walked into the laundry room, grabbed a kitchen towel and wiped up the mess. After tossing the towel in the sink, he opened the cupboard and pulled down a filter and the coffee. He shoved the filter into the basket and then readjusted it until it didn't look as if it were going to collapse.

With a quick yank he pulled the top off the coffee can, but it was a brand new can, filled to the brim. Coffee grounds flew through the air and landed around his feet on the floor.

What the hell was he doing? He slammed down the can, which expelled more grounds into the air. Oh he could kill Simone for putting him in such a mood and Cynthia for making him make her coffee. She should have just had sex with him.

Curtis retrieved the broom from the laundry room and swept up his mess. Finally, he managed to get grounds into the adjusted filter and pushed the button to start the brew.

When he heard Cynthia burst into laughter he spun around and narrowed his stare on her. This only forced her to laugh harder.

"You're a mess, you know that." She pulled a chair back from the kitchen table and sat down. She'd changed her shirt to one which wasn't as revealing, combed her hair, and he could smell the mint of the toothpaste. That was a sign, there'd be no sex.

Cynthia pushed another chair out with her foot. "Sit."

He grabbed hold of the chair, spun it backward, and then sat, resting his arms atop the back of the chair.

"So her cooking was this bad that it has you running to me in the middle of the night?"

"It's only eleven."

"I fell asleep at seven—it's the middle of the night for me."

He chuckled. This was why Cynthia was one of his dearest friends. She could sass him and it only made him want more.

"First off, she didn't cook. She enlisted my sister to cook."

"Oh, I had thought she'd at least burn something for your first." She smiled.

"I didn't even get to eat. I got called into work and ran out the door."

That caused Cynthia to laugh again. "I told her you were married to your job."

Curtis pushed to his feet. "You told her that?"

"She came at me the other day asking me if I was going to marry you. I laughed."

"You wouldn't marry me?"

"Hell no." She stood to meet him eye to eye. "You're married to your job. You love what you do. Next comes your family. If one of them needs you, you're there."

"That's how it's supposed to work."

"Right."

Now he was confused. What were they arguing about?

Cynthia moved past him and reached into the cupboard for two mugs. "My point is, Simone is looking for a fairytale."

"Well she was living that wasn't she?"

"Maybe, but she's here now. And she's set her sights on you."

Curtis pulled his fingers through his hair and sat down again. "I swear that she was trying to ask me to marry her during dinner."

Cynthia laughed again as she turned toward him with two full mugs of coffee. "I have a beer too if you'd rather."

"Still on call."

"Right."

He didn't like that tone, but it was well deserved.

"Anyway, I cut her off. I ran out the door." He didn't like how it was sounding.

Cynthia took a sip from her coffee. "So go back to her and wake *her* up."

He pushed the mug away and stood to pace the small kitchen. "I did go back. Stood there at the front door watching her cozy up with Sam on the couch."

"Cozy up? As in they were naked and doing it?" Her voice hadn't even quivered when she said it.

"No!" God she was making him crazy. "It was almost more intimate. He had his arm around her. Her head was on his chest. He covered her up with a blanket and kissed the top of her head."

"Yep, you're screwed. She's sunk her claws into him." The permanent grin on her face was pissing him off.

"You're joking with me? You think this is funny."

She sipped her coffee again. "I think it is hysterical. Sam isn't moving in on your territory."

"How do you know that?"

"Because I believe in him. It's me that has my claws in him, and I tell you what, I don't have any intentions on letting go."

"You? One man?"

This time Cynthia stood to meet him eye to eye. "Listen, Keller. If you're going to come into my home and point fingers you might as well leave. If I remember correctly you came seeking me out, not the other way around. If your little French kitten has you looking to lash out, hit the gym, hit the bar, hit a damn wall for all I care, but leave me out of it."

He couldn't even react. Cynthia had never talked to him like that before. Dear God, she was in love with Sam.

A smile formed on his lips. "Wow. I never thought I'd see you settle into one man."

"Likewise with you." She gave him a shove and then sat back down. "You're in love with Simone and you probably hurt her feelings when you walked out on her. Sam is a caring, compassionate man who was probably only giving her comfort."

When he thought about it that was exactly how it had looked too.

He would need to make it up to Simone, and probably to Cynthia too. He always hated when reality made sense and he didn't.

He knew what he'd do. He'd stop by the clinic tomorrow and take Simone some flowers. Every woman loved flowers, especially when the man in their life was a jerk. In a week he would have a full weekend off. Perhaps it was time to make sure he wasn't available to the hospital and he could take Simone away, nowhere fancy, but just the two of them.

If she had been trying to propose to him maybe he'd beat her to the punch. After all it was a man's job.

A sharp pain pierced his chest. What the hell was he thinking?

Did he want to get married? Did he want to marry Simone? It only made sense. He'd never loved anyone before. But marriage?

His own head spun now. Love. He could absolutely say he loved her, that scared him more than the thought of marriage, but then again there was a comfort in it too.

He chuckled to himself. Who would have thought he and Cynthia were ready to settle down? He guessed the friends with benefits gig was over.

CHAPTER 30

The next day Simone filed papers in the cabinets in the room designated for files. She appreciated the quiet of the job. Her mind was crowded with thoughts and the peace gave her time to consider what she was going to do.

Curtis needed to know about the baby. She wasn't sure he'd choose her over his job, but he needed to know.

She'd called him four times to see if he'd meet her after work, but all she got was his voice mail. It was nearing the end of the day for her and she figured if she hadn't heard back from him by the time she got home she'd call her father next.

"Room is open." She looked up from her stack of papers and saw Sam standing in the doorway. "C'mon, Monica is gone, we only have ten minutes to do this."

"Oh, the ultrasound. Right."

She put the stack of papers back into the folder she'd carried in, hurried back to her desk and slid them in her drawer. Her co-worker watched her a bit too intently so she gave her a smile and hurried off with Sam.

The room was dimly lit. There was only one bed and the machine occupying the room the size of a linen closet.

"Get up on the bed." Sam instructed as he pushed buttons on the keyboard attached to the large machine.

Simone did as he'd instructed.

"Now, lift your shirt up so I can see your stomach and roll down the waistband of your pants."

She gave him a hesitant nod and again did what he'd asked.

He took a towel and tucked it into the waist of her pants then ran his hand over her taunt stomach.

"Won't be long. Your about to pop."

"Pop?" Her voice cracked.

"Yeah, your baby bump is about to start showing. You have a cute little swell."

Simone felt the surge of tears begin to surface in her throat as Sam took the blue gel from the holder. He shook it and squeezed some on her stomach. She winced for the cold.

"Sorry. Usually it's warmed up, but there were no patients in here today."

Simone nodded as Sam returned the bottle and grabbed the wand. "Okay, are you ready to see this peanut?"

Her throat was so clogged with the tears she knew were going to break free she only nodded.

Sam set the wand on her stomach and a moment later she saw the first pictures of her baby.

"Oh, my." The tears broke free and there was no sucking them in. "I have never seen anything so precious in my life."

"Hold on let me see if I can get the face."

He managed the wand and then a perfect profile of the baby she and Curtis had created was there on the screen. His hand was near his face and he looked as though he hiccupped.

"Did you feel that?" Sam asked.

"Yes," she said through her tears. "Yes, I did. I can't believe this. I can't..." She couldn't speak anymore. She wanted to just stare at the image on the screen.

. . .

Curtis walked through the front door of the clinic and straight through the reception door. As giddy and stupid as he felt at that moment he wasn't so sure he wouldn't drop down on one knee and ask Simone to marry him.

He hid the flowers behind his back and walked directly to her office. There was no way to help the disappointment when he only saw the other girl she worked with sitting at her desk.

"I'm sorry to bother you. I'm looking for Simone Pierpont."

The woman raised her eyebrows at him. "She just took off with one of the nurses, Sam."

That didn't sit well with him, but he'd promised himself he wasn't going to get worked up. "Do you know when they'll be back?"

"Oh, who knows. They were being all secretive. She left her work in her desk and they ran off down the hall to the room by the bathroom."

That straightened Curtis' spine. He turned from her office, dropped the flowers in the trashcan in the hallway and headed to that room where she'd snuck off with Sam. He'd been a fool once, even twice, but there wasn't going to be a third time.

He grabbed hold of the door handle and pushed it open.

Sam's head shot up and Simone had let out a small scream, not one to cause alarm, but enough to let him know he'd gotten his point across.

But then the moment hit him—hit him hard. He noticed her on the table, her shirt up. Sam had an ultrasound wand on her stomach and on the screen there was the image of a baby.

God damn! Simone was pregnant!

CHAPTER 31

*T*he moment was frozen in time. His breath caught in his lungs and wouldn't move in or out. He could feel his head spin from the lack of oxygen.

The moment Sam stepped away from Simone, the image of the baby disappeared from the screen.

Simone sat up and only looked at him. Did she have nothing to say?

Heat vibrated through his body. He'd never been so angry in his entire life. He could feel the blood course through his veins and his jaw hurt from clenching his teeth together.

There should have been a million words to share with her, but they seemed to be stuck in his throat. Instead, he turned around and walked away.

He'd heard her call his name as he turned and walked down the hall and out of the clinic. Every muscle in his body ached as he hurried out to his truck. Of course, his heart ached most.

Oh, what and idiot he'd been to involve himself in her games. She must have thought he was some kind of fool to fall for her charm.

He started the truck and sped out of the parking lot.

So that was what her bumbling was all about last night. Talking about his family. She was using him to build a family for her baby. Well he wasn't interested. And he wasn't a fool anymore.

There was only one way to rid himself of Simone Pierpont and that was to send her packing.

Only one man could do that and Curtis was going to see to it that Zach made her go away.

MARY ELLEN SAT AT HER DESK—THE GUARDIAN TO ZACH'S PRIVATE world. When she'd seen Curtis walking toward his office she'd lifted her head and smiled, but he knew the look on his face spelled out danger and instead of waving him in, as she usually would, she stood quickly and barricaded the door by stepping in his way.

"Curtis, it's nice to see you."

"I need him."

She held up a hand. "He's on a very important phone call."

With all due respect to the woman who took care of his brother-in-law, she needed to get out of his way.

"Trust me, I won't make a sound."

He skirted around her and pushed his way into Zach's office.

Zach sat at his large desk the phone receiver to his ear. He head shot up when he saw Curtis walk into his office and then his eyes darted to Mary Ellen who shrugged her shoulders.

Zach continued his conversation as he gave Curtis a nod and Mary Ellen a wave, which she took as her signal to leave.

Curtis sat down on the leather couch and wrung his hands together while he waited.

He watched Zach. He was rubbing his temples listening to the person on the other end of the conversation. Whatever the phone call was about Zach was immersed in it and it was weighing heavy on him.

Curtis felt like an idiot for barging in. Simone wasn't Zach's responsibility either.

A moment later Zach leaned back, looked at the receiver in his hand and then hung up the phone, without a word.

"I guess he was done with me." He scrubbed his hands over his face and shifted his stare to Curtis.

There was an awkward silence between them, but Curtis was sure that Zach had something to say, and he was certain they were about initiate the same topic of conversation.

Zach pointed to the phone. "That was Monsieur Pierpont."

There was a tightening in Curtis' chest. "He ready for his princess back? I'm ready to send her packing."

Zach gnawed on his lip then tapped his fingers on the desk. "Seems as though she's called him, just a few moments ago. He's sending a plane for her."

"Good." Curtis stood and paced the small area between the desk and Zach's desk. "I know she's your dearest friend and all, but she's nothing but trouble. I'd feel better knowing she's as far away from Nashville, my friends, and my family as possible."

"What happened to you two working things out? I thought you were in love with her."

"I was wrong." He pressed his hands on the top of the desk and leaned on it. "So you know why she was turned away now?"

Zach pinched the bridge of his nose. "I don't mean to be rude, but I have more problems than your love life." He picked up a file on his desk and then tossed it back down. "Pierpont wants to do a build, but he's got an investor."

"So?" It was pissing Curtis off that Zach couldn't for just five minutes leave his business and talk about getting rid of Simone.

"The investor is Michael Hamilton."

"Are you kidding me?" His temper was boiling again. "What's wrong with that family? You don't do business with a woman beating bastard." He could feel the head beneath his collar. Just the mention of the name made him want to lash out.

He'd been there when Michael Hamilton had nearly killed his sister and her daughter. She'd given the baby away to hide her, but the man still came around.

He hooked his thumbs into his front pocket. "You're not doing the build are you?"

"No." The answer was firm. Zach sat back in his chair. "He's testing me. He wants to see if I'll sell out—or if I'm loyal to my family."

Curtis' mind shifted to Simone. "He doesn't seem to be too loyal to his own family, why is he worried about you?"

"It's a power trip."

"And that's all this was with Simone? She tripped up his power."

"I think so. I can't imagine what she did."

Curtis winced. Obviously Zach didn't know.

He wasn't sure it was his place to discuss it, but if anyone deserved to know that Simone Pierpont was as conniving as her father, it was Zach.

He took a breath to tell him about the baby when Mary Ellen burst through the door. "Security just called." Her voice was quick and sharp. She moved to the elevator in the corner of the office and pushed the button.

Zach must have noticed her concern. He jumped from his chair and followed her.

Mary Ellen shifted a look at Curtis and then back to Zach. "Simone is here." She hushed her voice, but there was enough panic in it that it hadn't quieted any. "She just crashed her car in the parking garage."

That gave Curtis' heart a start. As the door opened to the elevator he dashed across the office and stepped in. "Push the button, hurry."

Mary Ellen placed her hand on his arm. "I don't think it's too bad, they didn't ask for an ambulance."

Curtis turned and looked Zach square in the eye. "She's pregnant. We have to make sure she's okay."

The door closed and Zach turned to him, his eyes narrow and angry. "Run that by me again."

"Simone is pregnant. That's why she's in Nashville. That's why her father pushed her out."

He'd seen fear in Zach's eyes before—even hurt and desperation, but this was the first time he'd seen pure anger surge through his brother-in-law. "What have you done?"

"Me? Oh, this is far beyond me, pal."

"She told you that?"

"She didn't tell me squat!" His temper was rising and God help him he was still a man. If you attacked him personally he was going to come out swinging, but this was Zach, he couldn't do that.

When the door opened on the main floor of the parking garage, the three of them hurried out of the elevator and ran up the ramp until they saw the security car parked behind Simone's. She'd hit the cement barrier on the opposite side of the ramp.

Zach hurried to the car, but Curtis slowed. For the first time in his life, the medical first responder didn't react. He didn't want to see her. He didn't want to acknowledge her. He didn't want to feel.

The distance didn't matter. He could hear her cry—sob.

Zach's voice was soft, but Simone was still hysterical. He couldn't just stand there anymore.

Slowly, he walked toward the car. Zach was crouched down next to her, the car door open only slightly, confined by the concrete wall.

Zach stood and exchanged glances with Curtis. He walked toward him leaving Simone still sobbing in the car.

BERNADETTE MARIE

"You should look at her. She hit her head. She might need stitches."

That wasn't what he wanted to hear. He'd wanted her to just be miserable, not hurt. Oh, who was he kidding, he'd only wanted her gone so he wouldn't be miserable.

Upon Zach's request he walked to the car.

Simone sobbed and blood covered her forehead. There was a gash above her right eye. No doubt she'd hit her head on the steering wheel.

"Are you okay?"

"Do I look okay to you?" She brushed her hand under her nose. "I just need to get out of this car. I have a…"

"A flight. I know."

He heard her sigh. "Curtis, go away."

"C'mon. Let me get you to the hospital and get that closed up. Then I'll get you to your flight, personally."

He wasn't sure if it was the nature of his job or his upbringing that had him giving her compassion, but when the urge to kiss her to calm her took over he quickly squashed the idea by remembering that he didn't love her anymore. How could he love someone who wanted to use him and his family?

He took time to assess her as he helped her from the car. Aside from a few bumps and bruises, and of course the cut on her head, she looked fine. He agreed, she didn't need an ambulance.

Curtis held onto her arms as she skirted the back side of the car. She shook and it resonated through his skin.

"Now, stay right here with Zach for a moment. I have to get my truck."

"Wait," Zach said as he pulled his keys from his pocket. "My car is right there. It might be easier for her to get into."

Curtis let out a breath. As much as he hated to agree with him, he did so with a nod. Of course, it also meant he'd have to return the car and answer back to Zach.

He pulled his keys out of his pocket and handed them to Zach in exchange for Zach's car keys.

"Zach, perhaps you should take me. I do not think Curtis should drive me," Simone spoke through her sobs.

"He'll take good care of you," Zach promised. "Now, go." He moved in and kissed her on the cheek and then leaned in to her and whispered in her ear. "If you need anything you call me. I'll miss you."

"He called you already?"

Zach nodded.

"He still hates me."

Zach scanned a look over her and his eyes brightened. "He has no reason to. Now go with Curtis.

Curtis helped Simone toward Zach's car.

There wasn't a single word between them as he helped her into the car and then climbed in and started the car. But her sobs had increased.

Against his better judgment, he turned to her. "How did you hit that wall? How do you crash in a parking garage?" He'd meant to ask if she needed anything, but this was what flew from his lips.

"I got confused. Everything confused me." She wiped at her eyes and then looked at her hands which had blood on them. "Oh, this is horrible."

"It's not that bad."

"It is not on *your* face," she spat back. "Just get me out of here. You can drop me on the corner. Just go so Zach cannot see me."

Curtis put the car in reverse and drove out of the parking garage.

He swallowed the lump in his throat and cleared it to speak. He only had a few more hours with Simone Pierpont in his life, he could show some compassion. "After I get your head fixed, and I think it'll only need a butterfly stitch, I'll look at the baby and make sure he's okay."

She tensed, he noticed that, but she didn't look at him. He gripped the steering wheel tighter as her sobs came harder. If she'd wanted to talk she couldn't have and now, her face was flushed red and her breathing was increasingly heavy. He was afraid she'd hyperventilate.

CHAPTER 32

$\mathcal{C}$urtis was relieved when they pulled into the parking lot at the hospital and it wasn't too full. Perhaps he could get her in and out without too much trouble. He couldn't remember being less comfortable around anyone in his entire life.

He helped her out of the car and escorted inside, past those waiting in the waiting room, and quickly past the nurses' station, but they hadn't snuck past Cynthia.

"Simone! What happened?" She hopped up from her seat and followed them to a bed where Curtis closed the curtain in around them.

"It is nothing really."

Curtis washed his hands and turned right into Cynthia. Now he had two crazed women on his hands.

"Nothing? You're bleeding." She shoved past him and washed her hands.

Curtis went through the cart looking for the items he needed to get Simone fixed up. Cynthia, on the other hand, was doing all the fussing over her.

She reached past him for the sterile water bottle and towels.

Then she shoved him aside for a pair of gloves, all the while talking up a storm as if she were the one who was nervous about something. Simone, on the other hand, hadn't said anything.

"Okay, lay back," she ordered Simone. "This is going to be cold." She placed the towel under the cut and over Simone's eyes and began to wash out the small wound.

What hadn't gone unnoticed by Curtis was the fact she'd laid her hands on her stomach and for the first time he noticed the very small swell.

He fisted his hands and then opened them reminding himself she'd be out of his life in a few hours.

Cynthia continued to clean out the wound and talk to keep Simone calm, but Simone lay quietly.

Finally Curtis took a seat on the stool next to the bed. He laid all the materials he needed on the tray next to him. The wound wasn't bad. Head wounds always looked worse than they were because they bled so much.

"Did you hit your head on the steering wheel?" he asked.

"Yes," she said very softly, nearly inaudible.

"Simone, how did you do this? You couldn't have been going too fast," Cynthia chimed in as Curtis opened the package of bandages.

"I was just worked up and not paying attention," again her voice was soft, almost inaudible.

Curtis lifted the bandages from their protective case with tweezers. Cynthia moved in beside him to help secure their placement and a moment later he tore off his gloves. "Done."

"I'm glad you didn't hurt yourself worse. You can still dance with this," Cynthia said and they both looked at her. "Oh, c'mon, I heard you two had a great time. I want to go out again."

Curtis watched as Simone's eyes lowered and he stood up from the stool. "I'll be right back."

He walked out of the curtained area in search of a sonogram machine and realized Cynthia was right on his heels.

"She's bawling like a baby in there. What the hell did you do to her?"

"How is it that everyone assumes I'm the reason for her misery?" He opened the door to another room and saw the machine he was looking for. "She's old enough to have made her own mistakes. I have nothing to do with her."

"Nothing to do with her? I thought you two worked things out. I thought you were in love with her. I thought you were going back after you pissed me off and working on not being such an ass." Cynthia stood at the door and watched him. "What's the machine for?"

He huffed out an angry breath. "If you must know, she's pregnant and I promised her I'd check on the baby."

Cynthia stepped into the room and let the door shut behind her. "She's what?"

"Oh, please. You see this every day of your life. Simone is pregnant."

"You're having a baby?"

He wrapped the cord around his hand. "Not me. Her. I have nothing to do with this."

"She told you it was someone else's baby?"

"She didn't tell me anything." And that was getting to him more than any part of her antics. Even when he said he'd check on the baby she hadn't said a word.

"Curtis," she placed a gentle hand on his arm, "you need to talk to her. Why would she have come here if it wasn't your baby?"

"You don't know her. She comes from a conniving family and she's just posh enough to think she needs a daddy for her baby. What better man than one who has a gracious family around him all the time."

"I don't think she'd use you."

"Oh, yeah? She's been around the block, honey. I'm sure there are a lot more men who have claim to that baby than me."

"I could slap you." She stepped up to him and stood there nearly chest to chest. "Just because a woman has been a bit free with herself doesn't mean she can't love the right man. Things happen, Curtis. Maybe if you'd give her a moment you'd see that."

"She seems to be in a much better relationship with your boyfriend than she is with me. Maybe we should talk to him about this. Maybe he's the daddy."

At that point Cynthia did slap him right across the cheek and it stung.

He gritted his teeth against the pain. "Get out of my way. I'm going to check on her and then take her to the airport. She's already called her daddy and he's sending a plane for his princess. My charity work here is done."

He pulled the machine past Cynthia and pushed it down the hall to the curtained off area where Simone had been, but now she was gone.

CHAPTER 33

*T*he only thing Simone could hope for was that by the time she landed in Paris all of her tears would be dry forever, but for now, alone on her father's charted jet, she'd cry.

For a moment at the hospital she thought there might have been a chance to salvage what had gone so badly wrong. She'd never intended on Curtis finding out she was pregnant in such a horrific way. He hadn't even asked any questions, he'd just turned to leave. Perhaps he was more volatile a personality than she'd thought. Just because all the other Kellers were sound minded didn't mean he was.

Perhaps that was good to know now, but still she would have thought he'd have said something. The only mention he'd even made was that he'd check on *her* baby.

The tears kept pouring down her cheeks and her head pounded where the strips of fabric held her cut closed. Oh, she must have looked like an idiot crashing into the wall at in Zach's building. That hadn't gone as planned either. The phone call to her father where she cried like a baby was about the only thing that had gone right. He'd said *I told you so* and sent for a plane.

She pulled the small lap blanket from the empty seat next to her and covered herself up. Her body shivered, not from the temperature of the air, but from the hateful words she'd overheard Curtis say to Cynthia.

He thought she'd run out of the room and skipped out on him, but not until after he'd left the hospital. She'd waited in the restroom until it was clear to walk out without being seen.

He had some lessons to learn about bedside manner. If you were going to talk so loudly that you could be heard from the bathroom across the hall, perhaps you shouldn't be a doctor.

She'd only needed to go to the restroom, she didn't know she'd find that Curtis thought the baby was someone else's and that she was trying to force him to be the father.

Well obviously, he was not father material.

She'd be better off in Paris with her father's money and her mother's strange empathy than with Curtis, who only thought of her as a tramp who got in some trouble.

The tears began to dry as she reclined in her seat, but the small flutter in her stomach couldn't be ignored. The baby was moving and it was just another moment Curtis would miss in the life of his child.

SIMONE CERTAINLY WAS SURPRISED TO SEE HER MOTHER WAITING for her when she arrived in Paris.

The tears were back when her mother lifted her arms and Simone hurried to her and accepted the embrace.

"Darling, you look terrible." Her mother pulled back and looked her over. "Are these pajamas? And, oh, what happened to your head? Simone, you never should have left France, dear. Look at you."

Simone swallowed hard. The comfort of a hug should have made her feel better, just as the one from Sam the other night had. But in her mother's grasp she felt small and insignificant.

Beatrice, wasn't mother material, and never had been. She

never asked how her daughter's day was or planned for birthday parties or sleepovers. Not once in all the years that Simone lived away at schools did her mother send her a care package, but Audrey Benson had.

Simone climbed into her mother's awaiting car.

"I did not expect you to pick me up."

"Your father had some business. I suppose he could not be bothered. He phoned my assistant and I arranged to be here for you, darling." She gave her another glance and the corners of her mouth turned downward. "We should stop and buy you some new clothes. Those are hideous."

"Mother, I have no money."

"Your father will pay me back. He had better." And that was the way Beatrice thought and it angered Simone.

"The clothes I have on now are fine and very comfortable. I would really prefer to just sleep for a spell."

"I would have thought Zachary Benson would have taken much better care of you than this." She motioned her hand in the air as if to ward away and evil the clothes might emit. "I am very disappointed in him."

"In Zachary? Mother do you even know why I left Paris?"

"Darling, you leave all the time. That is joy of being an heir to an oil fortune."

Hearing those words drip from her mother's tongue nearly made Simone sick. There was no pride in knowing that when her father died she'd have everything he'd worked for. Just the opposite. Money didn't buy happiness, she'd learned that first hand. At that moment she would have giving up everything, again, just to go back to her small office, her dank apartment, and to even have Curtis hate her in person if she didn't have to be faced with the shallowness of her own mother. But she'd left Nashville—run away. She was a coward with her tail between her legs.

Her mother's new home was an hour from the airport.

Simone was impressed, not in the house, or where it sat, but in the fact that her mother had made such a trip to pick her up.

They had made one stop in route so that Simone could use the restroom and purchase a toothbrush. At that point, her mother took it upon herself to purchase an outfit she felt Simone would look much better in. She'd been told to change into it right there in the store and her mother then threw away the set of scrubs Cynthia had given her.

When the driver parked the car, Simone reached for the door handle to climb out. Her mother cleared her throat and gave her a stern look. Simone sat back until the door was opened by the driver and her mother climbed out first.

Yes, she certainly would have had a fit had she seen her climb out of Curtis' truck only nights earlier and not let him walk her to the door.

Just as in all her mother's other homes, with other husbands, Simone had a room. In comparison to the apartment she shared with Sam, it was a penthouse suite.

"The clothes you left in my old house are in your closest, though you look as though you might have put on a few pounds. Not to worry, I'll call my trainer and we can get you back in shape."

"Mother, I am not gaining weight that I have to work off."

"Darling, I know how they eat in the States. Trust me, Pierre will have you looking as good as you did at Christmas. Oh, you were stunning."

Did? Were? It had to stop. Her mother had to understand that things were different now.

"Mother, I am pregnant."

Her mother's eyes first flashed with humor, but when Simone said nothing else anger settled in them.

"Pregnant? Simone, how?"

Simone cocked her head to the side and her mother's spine straightened.

"Oh, I know how. But you are not married. What will we do?"

Simone's chest ached. How had she been born to this woman? She longed for Tennessee and a moment with Audrey Benson. Perhaps even better would be to have a slice of pie at Emily Keller's table. The thought nearly had her laughing, but she actually feared the small, fiery French woman who stood before her in a panic that her adult daughter was going to have her own child.

Her mother composed herself. "And who is this child's father?"

"Doctor Curtis Keller."

Her mother searched for recognition, but she had no idea who Curtis was. Not once after Simone had left him stranded on that yacht had her mother paid one bit of attention to her when she'd pined for him.

"Doctor?"

Knowing that was all she heard sent Simone into a rage. "I should have stayed there. You are no better than my father, who cut me off and sent me away."

"You are being foolish. He would never do that."

"Really?" Simone fisted her hands on her hips. "Tell me, mother, are you not the slightest bit embarrassed by what I have told you? I mean, I am *in trouble*," she whispered the last part.

"Simone…"

"I am having a baby out of wedlock and the father does not think the baby is his. He too has turned me away. Are you not proud of me now?"

A crease formed in her mother's forehead. "We can have this taken care of."

"This isn't a ripped dress that can be mended. I am having a baby."

"Then we will find you a husband."

The first laugh broke free. And then the second. Before long they began to roll straight from Simone's stomach. "Mother, if the father of my baby did not want me, why would anyone else?"

"It just is not right."

Simone walked to the bed near the window and fell back on it. "Do you know what I did when I was in Tennessee? I got a job."

"This is no time to joke, Simone."

"I am not joking. I got a job in a medical clinic run by the government."

She could see the color drain from her mother's face and there was some merit in knowing she was causing it.

"Working there showed me that women did not need men to take care of them. They could be brave and strong and raise children all on their own."

"That is foolish."

"No, really, mother. I helped a woman, her name was Regina. Her husband had beaten her and she had a small son. I listened to her. Spent time with her. I helped to get her a job and even gave her my sixteenth birthday earrings so she could pawn them and get a place to stay away from her husband. Diamonds like that could buy her food and shelter for days."

"Your father gave you those earrings." Her mother swayed. "I feel faint."

Simone stood quickly and helped her to the bed where she sat down. Simone knelt down before her.

"Mother, I will be fine"

"I am embarrassed for you, Simone," she said in a whisper much like Simone had earlier.

"Then you are not who I thought you were, and neither am I."

Pride swelled inside of her as it had the day she worked for the first time. It bubbled over as it had when she'd seen Regina feel a bit of pride in herself because Simone had given her the tools to move on. Her mind traveled to the look on Curtis' face when he'd brought her the plant for her desk and he was proud of her too.

Why was she wasting her time at her mother's trying to justify that she was a grown woman, who now had a mission to raise her child with love and compassion, which money couldn't buy.

She'd need time, and she'd need money too, but in Paris she could have both. When her baby was born, she would leave the confinement of her parents' world and raise her baby the way *she* wanted to.

CHAPTER 34

*C*urtis' way of dealing with things was to get lost. But because of his obligations this meant only going as far as his apartment and refusing to answer his phone unless it was the hospital paging him with an emergency.

He'd had an earful from Cynthia the moment they realized Simone was gone, as if smacking him across the face hadn't been enough. If she talked to him again he'd be surprised. Funny how the woman in his life had bonded with the woman he thought he'd wanted in his life and now he was the odd man out.

The only reason he'd answered the phone when Zach called was because he thought he'd have some information on Simone. But no, he'd called to chew him out too.

Who cared what everyone else thought. Simone got herself into trouble, why did she assume it was his responsibility to get her out of it?

He plopped himself down on his couch and kicked his feet up on the coffee table.

With the remote in his hand he sat there staring at the TV, which he'd never turned on. Instead his mind replayed the moment he'd walked in on Simone and Sam. The image of the baby on the screen had hit a nerve. He shouldn't care, he didn't want to care. But damn it he did.

He dropped his feet to the floor and threw the remote on the couch next to him.

If the baby were his, she would have told him. Simone wasn't the kind of person to skirt issues. She'd been plenty blunt with him about the number of men she'd been with, there must have been a reason for that too.

Curtis dropped his head back against the back of the couch. The part that hurt the most was that no matter how upset he was, he still loved her, and he wanted that feeling to go away.

IT HAD BEEN TWO WEEKS SINCE SIMONE WALKED OUT OF CURTIS' life. It had also been that long since he'd seen Cynthia. What could it hurt on a beautiful Sunday morning, to try an mend a long and meaningful friendship? He'd trekked across the grounds from the hospital to the clinic on his lunch break to say hello.

Luckily, she was on break, sitting outside at the concrete tables next to Sam. She glowered at him when she saw him walking toward her.

"Didn't suppose you'd come out of hiding for a long time." She pulled a chip from the bag and bit down on it.

"Can't hide forever." He sat down at the table and gave Sam a nod. "Hey, Sam, how's it going?"

"Can't complain."

"So what are you doing here?" Cynthia was more direct, but that had always been one of her more charming qualities.

"I just thought I'd drop by to say hi."

"Hi."

There was a bitterness in her tone. He'd lost a lot more than Simone that day she'd walked away from him, again. He'd lost the respect of his dearest friend.

Sam wadded up his trash. "I'd better get going." He turned to Cynthia. "I'll pick you up after work."

She gave him a nod, but it said much more.

"See ya 'round, Curtis."

"Sure. Hey, Sam, if you need me to come by and get Simone's things out of your place let me know. I know you probably need to get it rented out."

"No hurry. I got a check in the mail the other day for rent for a few months. I figure she'll be back." He gave them a wave and walked away.

"Simone sent a check?" His voice had risen higher than he'd anticipated.

"Someone sent a money order. Not her specifically. My guess is Zach."

"She's talked to Zach?"

Cynthia rested her arms on the table and inched in closer to him. "Did you come over here to hound me for information? What makes you think I'd give it to you?"

He'd never been uneasy around Cynthia before. He didn't like the distance between them now.

"No, actually until Sam said that, I hadn't planned on mentioning her at all."

"Standup guy you are, Keller." She stood and gathered her trash.

He stood and followed her to the trash can. "What did I do?"

"She needed you and you let her down."

"I let her down? She walked out on me, again."

"You didn't give her a chance. You're never going to know your child and that doesn't sit well with me."

There was a sharp pain in his chest. He reached his hand to his breastbone and rubbed it away. "My baby? She told you it was my baby?"

"Go away, Keller."

She turned from him but he reached for her. "Listen, she told me she'd been with all these men. Rich, influential men. How am I supposed to know this is my baby?"

Cynthia's eyes softened. "Because you love her and you know in your heart that's why she came this far and why she even kept the baby. Look what she had to lose to do that."

Curtis rubbed the heat at the back of his neck. That piece of logic didn't settle well with him.

"Why wouldn't she just tell me then?"

"Perhaps she wanted to prove to you that she could do this. The world only sees heiress. Some of us see a woman wanting to prove that she's worthy of everything."

Cynthia placed her hand on his shoulder. "Go talk to Zach. See if he's talked to her. Maybe now that she's back in Paris she's come to terms with who she is. Maybe money and prestige is what she was missing. And if the baby isn't yours, maybe she's told the father."

"But you don't think that's the case?"

"No, I don't."

She moved in closer to him and kissed him on the cheek. "Go get her. You're miserable."

She knew him best. He was absolutely miserable.

CHAPTER 35

*S*imone had settled back into her father's house as comfortably as she could. He didn't parade her around or take her in public. In fact, he hardly spoke to her at all. No matter what, she'd embarrassed him.

He'd offered her a portion of her trust fund back and had sent someone to purchase her tasteful maternity clothing, in case she was seen. But not once had he said he was glad she'd come back.

A grown woman, and still she was treated like a child, but she needed the security of his home and his money for her child.

The swell of her stomach was obvious now as she lay in her childhood bed. At night, especially, she could feel her baby move, but she was still lonely.

Since that day she'd walked out of the hospital, she hadn't talked to anyone in the States. It was as if they had forgotten her, but she knew that wasn't true. Simone Piermont had come and gone her entire life. When she needed company, she took someone home with her. When she needed a friend, she always landed at Zach's house. And when a real man fell in love with her and took care of her—she stranded him.

The baby moved, reminding her of her biggest mistake of all. If she'd gone directly to Curtis and told him about the baby, she might just be wrapped in his arms, not hiding in her father's house.

She rolled onto her side and looked out her window as the drapes blew in the night breeze. She missed her waterbed in her tiny bedroom back at Sam's. What she wouldn't give to be there again.

CURTIS PULLED UP IN FRONT OF HIS SISTER'S HOUSE. HE HADN'T realized that the seasons were changing as quickly as they were. The leaves on the trees, which lined the drive, were falling to the ground and there was a cool nip in the air.

His mind had been otherwise occupied, he guessed.

The front door of the house opened as Curtis parked his truck and climbed out. The sight before him had nearly buckled his knees. His nephew stood there, unsupported, waddling toward him.

It affected him more than he ever thought it would. How could one moment in time be so precious and steal a man's breath?

He hurried up the steps toward Tyler who continued his waddle into the waiting arms of his uncle.

Curtis scooped him up and planted a kiss on his cheek. "We're going to have to get you some new squeaky shoes so Mama knows where you are at all times."

"Maybe you could come over on your next day off and hang all the gates in all the doorways for his mama. That would be most helpful," Regan said from the doorway.

"I'd be happy to." He carried Tyler into the house, stopping long enough to give his sister a peck on the cheek.

He noticed immediately that her body was changing. The

swell of her stomach was very pronounced now, even though she was only halfway through her pregnancy.

Immediately, he thought of Simone.

He didn't know specifics of Simone's pregnancy, but he knew she was nearly as far along as Regan. She'd be showing now too. He figured there was no more hiding it from the world.

What could Monsieur Pierpont think of that?

When he thought about it that way a knot of regret formed in his stomach. He knew he didn't think much of it at all and if he had Simone wouldn't have shown up on Regan's front step in the first place.

What could it possibly be like to be a grown woman and not have anyone to believe in you? Well, he thought, she'd always had Zach.

As Curtis walked further into the house he saw Zach sitting in his office, the phone to his ear, and a look of absolute concentration on his face. Even after business hours, the man worked hard.

He continued on to the kitchen, his sister close behind.

"How are you feeling lately?" He asked her as he set Tyler on the floor near a small pile of his toys.

"Much better. Aside from the fact that I don't sleep real well and my back is already starting to hurt. But I'd take my size changing in lieu of getting sick every day."

He helped Regan set the table and finish up dinner. He was happy to see only three settings on the table. There had been some fear that dinner at Regan's would turn into an entire family affair with his brother and their parents. As this was the first time he'd come out of hiding long enough to be near his family in nearly a month, he didn't want to have to face them all in one night.

Zach joined them as Regan set a plate of fried chicken on the table. Curtis noticed his eyes. He was preoccupied with something, probably something to do with the phone call he'd taken in his home office.

Curtis appreciated his brother-in-law. Though as a doctor he had to maintain a certain amount of patience, Zach Benson had more.

When Curtis tended to a patient they usually were under his care until they were well enough to go home or move to another area of the hospital. His commitment to that person, though it be life or death, was usually a few days at most. But with Zach Benson, everything was set up to take years and years. A build didn't just happen. There were plans, buys, investors, more plans, and then construction could take years itself. How he managed that everyday, Curtis would never understand.

Regan sat Tyler in his high chair and took the seat next to her husband. She rested her hand on his, Curtis noticed as he helped himself to chicken.

"Everything okay?" He heard her whisper as Tyler beat the table with a spoon.

"It will be," Zach said as quietly.

CHAPTER 36

*T*he dinner conversation was kept to Eduardo's job with Zach, Arianna's current role on Broadway, the invitation the next evening to see Clara play at her guitar recital, and Tyler's play date at the park. Nothing had been mentioned about Simone and he wanted to find comfort in that, but he didn't.

When they were finished eating, Curtis began to gather plates. If nothing else, his mother had taught him to be a gracious guest, even in the home of his sister.

"Curtis, let's talk in my office," Zach had finally said as if he hadn't noticed him helping Regan clear the table.

He exchanged glances with his sister, who only nodded and brushed him away with her hand.

Zach was already pacing the small office when Curtis walked in.

"Shut the door," he said and Curtis did so.

There was an uneasiness in the room. It wasn't something Curtis had felt since his father had wanted to know how the gash on the car door happened. In hindsight, Curtis had hoped that was the last time he'd have been so uncomfortable in the presence of another man.

Zach continued to pace the room.

"What did you want to talk about?" Curtis finally broke the silence.

Zach turned toward him, scrubbing his hand over his face. "I received a phone call before dinner, and now I'm torn between my commitment to my family, my loyalty to my friend, and the benefits to my company."

Curtis narrowed his eyes on Zach. "All that said, I assume this is all about Pierpont Oil?"

Zach shrugged. "It's all about Simone."

Curtis decided that was worse, but at least it made sense as to why he was sitting there like a child about to get a beating.

Zach finally sat in the chair that faced Curtis. He clasped his hands together and looked up at him.

"How did you know she was pregnant? When did she tell you?"

"She didn't." Now Curtis was up on his feet pacing the room. "I walked in on her and Sam doing an ultrasound."

"And that's it? Then what?"

"Then what? Then I showed up at your office and she crashed the car."

Zach sat back in his chair. "She didn't tell you any of this before?"

"No." His temper was rising. "Listen, I know the princess is your dearest friend, and I realize I have strained that relationship. I'm sorry."

"My question to you is what are you going to do about it?"

Curtis felt his jaw tense and the heat under the collar of his shirt rose. "Me? Why is this my responsibility?"

"Because it's your baby." Zach had stood, and as Curtis turned they were now eye to eye.

"Be logical for just one moment." He took a step back. "If she

BERNADETTE MARIE

came here to tell me she was having my baby why didn't she just do that? Why play all these games? Why get a job? Why get an apartment? She's pulling us both along, Zach."

"She wouldn't do that."

"Really? She's yet to be very straight forward with me about anything, except when she told me I was just one of many men she'd had on that yacht."

For the first time since Curtis had met Zach, he actually feared him when he turned to the office door and released the curtain that would shield the glass on the French door, effectively blocking out the world. When Zach turned back toward him there was a fire in his eyes and Curtis was sure one of them were going to walk out of that room with a black eye. Worse yet, he was sure it was going to be him.

"I've been around enough to see you work your way with the ladies. I've seen you string out Cynthia for years."

Curtis held his hands up in defense. "Now wait, that's our agreement."

"No matter your agreement, at what point in your adult life have you gone to bed with someone with intentions of waking up with them for the rest of your life?"

Curtis opened his mouth to speak only to close it again without an answer.

"I don't care what she's done in the past. Simone Pierpont is not a vindictive brat. She might not be wise in the ways of the world beyond her front door, but she was trying."

Curtis would have had to agree if Zach had given him a moment to chime in, but instead he continued his verbal assault.

"If she says this baby is yours then I have no reason to doubt her."

"You talked to her? You actually talked to her and she said that?"

"She was the phone call I took before dinner."

"And she said that the baby is mine?"

Zach nodded.

Curtis could feel the blood begin to drain from his face. Though the thought that the baby might be his had crossed his mind, it had never seemed logical until Zach said it.

The image on the screen of the baby flashed in his mind. He'd been drawn to it as if he'd known the unborn, unseen baby.

Suddenly he felt the need to sit down, as if the weight of his body could no longer be supported by his legs. The change in Regan's appearance had made him think of Simone immediately. If that was his baby, he was missing out on everything.

And to hell with it, if it wasn't his baby—well it could be. The point in it all was he was in love with Simone. He'd been in love with her since the moment they'd danced at Carlos' wedding. Nothing had changed, no matter how upset he was with her.

Not once in his life had he thought about settling down with anyone. Curtis Keller was a doctor and that was all. But there was more to him, and he knew that now. He wanted to love one woman for the rest of his life. To wake in Simone's arms every morning and fall asleep in them as well was exactly what he wanted.

Pangs of guilt washed over him when he thought about her going through her pregnancy alone. That should be something they did together. He had to get to her.

He stood to tell Zach his plan. He had to get to Paris, but the realization hit him, what if she turned him away, again?

Did it matter?

"She's miserable, Curtis." He walked toward him and rested his hand on Curtis' shoulder. "She'd rather be here and have you hate her, than to be there and miserable."

Curtis looked at his brother-in-law and thought hard about what he was about to say. "I don't hate her. I love her."

"I was banking on that." He turned and picked up the phone on his desk. "I can't believe Simone Pierpont wants to live in that dump of an apartment and work for the government, but she does. I'll call Mary Ellen and get her a plane ticket."

Curtis swallowed hard. "Someone should be there for her, don't you think? Fly to Paris, I mean."

Zach smiled. "I think she'd appreciate that."

CHAPTER 37

*S*imone's decision had been made and the phone call placed. She was leaving Paris for good, and this time she wasn't going to let her father have a say with how she lived her life.

She'd had a job, and that had given her more pride than the name Pierpont ever had. Even though she might not have that job anymore, she'd find another.

Standing in front of her father's desk in his office, Simone still felt like a child. He looked her over, his arms crossed in front of his broad chest.

"You will be back. You do not have what it takes to be a common working woman. You and your baby will suffer."

Simone stood with her arms to her side, her designer maternity dress showing off her growing stomach. "This is what I want."

"And you will pay greatly for it."

"I want my child to have both of his parents near him. That is important."

He tapped his fingers against his arms. "I am disappointed in

Zachary for letting you get involved with that doctor. This is a big mistake."

"Zachary had nothing to do with this." How could he even think such a thing?

"How long, Simone? How long before you are back on my phone begging me for my money again?"

Her heart squeezed painfully. "That is not what I have done."

"No? You think there is more to it?"

"I wanted my family."

His lips pursed as if he didn't understand her need. That was usually how it went. He thought about his money and his empire long before he took his daughter into consideration.

Just as she took a breath to give her father a piece of her mind, she could hear a commotion in the hallway. Her father stood from behind his desk.

"Sir, you can't go in there." The housekeeper's voice echoed down the hall.

Simone's heart thumped in her chest. He'd come. He'd come for her. He'd come for them.

"Let me into the office." His voice was muffled.

He did love her. He wanted them. She was ready to cry. Curtis Keller had come for her.

Simone's hands shook and she clenched them as the door to the office opened. The housekeeper stepped inside.

"I told him…"

A moment later he walked through the door. Simone sucked in a breath, let it out slow, and turned toward the door to see her savior's face.

Her father stood from behind his desk. "Zachary Benson, I do not have time for childish games."

"Monsieur Pierpont, it's not a game," he said as he walked into the room, not even offering his hand for her father to shake. Zach looked at her. "Are you okay?"

She couldn't speak. She could only nod.

Her father walked around the desk to face Zach. "She is always playing games. Now they have caught up to her. Look at her. I am disgraced."

Zach did look at her, and he smiled. "She is beautiful."

Her father chuckled. "You cannot always rescue her when she is mad at me."

"I always will. She is as close as I have to a sister. I will always protect her."

"And you think I am a threat to her?"

"No, sir. I don't mean any disrespect. But she's a grown woman, having a child. She deserves some respect for that."

"I blame you." Her father's finger came up in accusation. "You involve her in these common people, and now she has disgraced my name."

Simone's hand slipped into Zach's and he gave it a squeeze. "I'm very proud of this child she carries. You couldn't find a better family to be born into."

"*Her* family should have been good enough. Someone who was of the same cloth as her."

"I think she's done just fine." He shifted his gaze to her. "C'mon. You are part of my family. You have always been part of my family."

He started toward the door, her hand still in his.

"Zachary, if you leave with my daughter I will no longer help fund any of your builds."

Zach stopped and turned. "Again, I mean no disrespect, and you have been of great help over the years, but my firm is doing well. I will be fine without your investments."

"You are hurting yourself. I have an investor in Nashville."

Zach's hand tightened around hers and she wasn't sure he knew how hard his grip was. "I will never build for any organization that deems Michael Hamilton as a worthy investor."

Her father's lips pursed. "Simone, if you walk away you do not come back."

"Good bye, father." She released Zach's hand and walked out of her father's office for the very last time.

CHAPTER 38

*S*omewhere over the Atlantic, Simone finally felt as though she could breath. Zach had sat very quietly in the first class seat next to her.

For the first hour of their flight back to America, she was sick to her stomach. The second hour her hands shook until she tucked them under her to keep them still. She'd tried to sleep for the next few hours, but it was no use. She couldn't rest, there was a new world ahead of her again, and this time there was no turning back. There was also the realization that she sat next to Zachary on a flight back to the states, and not Curtis.

Zach waved down the flight attendant. "Can I get a bloody Mary and a cup of tea for my girl?"

The flight attendant nodded and walked away.

"Your girl?"

He patted her arm with his hand. "You've always been my girl and always will be, *mon ami.*"

There was a sadness in it for her. "And Regan?"

"Is my life."

Why she ever thought there would be any different answer, she wasn't sure. She didn't love Zachary, in fact now that she'd felt love, she realized she never had loved him in the way that she loved Curtis.

The flight attendant returned with their drinks. Zach lowered the tray tables and set the drinks atop of them as the flight attendant walked away.

"I know what's wrong with you."

Simone shifted in her seat. "Something is wrong with me?"

"You're upset that Curtis wasn't the one who walked through your father's office."

It would figure she was that transparent to him.

"I am sorry. I am glad you came for me, I truly am."

"I thought you'd like to know you still have your job at the clinic."

"I do not deserve that. I walked away from my responsibilities."

He was smiling at her. "You changed lives while you were there. Did you know Regina has been working steady? Her son has been in day care at the firm and I checked up on him. He's a cute little guy."

Tears began to well in her eyes. "That was you're doing."

"No. Without you stepping in to help her, she would have been home when that man of hers was released, and probably would have been beaten again. You gave her a new start. You gave her hope. You gave her the chance to move on with her life. You, Simone, have a gift and Marsha knew that. Curtis made sure she knew."

Her lips began to tremble. "Curtis made sure I still had my job?"

Zach nodded.

She found that hard to believe that Curtis would stand up for her at all. It only made the tears begin to fall. "What am I going to do, Zachary?"

"You've taken the first step. You've managed to almost make it through your thirties, and now have become an adult."

She slapped his arm and laughed through the tears. "This is going to be the hardest thing I've ever done."

"Aren't you ready for that?"

She took a deep breath her tears begin to dry. "I am ready for that. I am very ready for that."

"Trust me, sweetie." He took her hand in his and kissed it. "Regan and I are here for you. And I know for a fact we are not the only ones."

AS ZACH DROVE DOWN THE STREET TO HER APARTMENT, SIMONE began to feel the same sense of pride and peace she'd felt when she'd left Paris on her quest to prove to Curtis Keller that she could be something other than a pretty face. Now there were no secrets. The swell of her stomach made that perfectly clear. The father of her child might not want to love her, but she was sure he'd be a good father. What more could she ask?

Not only did she have her job and her home, the dearest friend she'd ever had was seated next to her. She knew if he'd have flown to Paris and spoken to her father as he had, he'd never leave her and her baby in need.

But Simone was also sure no one would ever have to assist her again. The moment she and Zach walked out of her father's house, she knew she'd never be back. And if she did go back, things would be different. She would be a mother and her image of that relationship, between a parent and a child, would be different—even with her own parents.

She could do this. Her life was hers to live and she'd never been so excited about the unknown ever in her life.

Zach pulled up in front of her apartment and parked the car.

"Go on in. I'll get your bags," he said.

She gave him a nod and climbed out of the car.

The flight had been excruciatingly long. One thing was for

sure, until after the baby was born, she wasn't going to sit that long on an airplane again.

Slowly she walked up the front steps to her front door. She slid her key into the lock and then pushed it open. The apartment was quiet. Sam was at work, which meant she'd have time to settle in.

Perhaps she'd make him dinner. Or at least try to.

Simone walked down the small hall to her bedroom. The door was closed. She turned the knob and slowly opened it.

It was dark, the blinds were closed, but there was something not right.

She reached for the switch and turned on the light.

The room was empty.

Her bed was gone. The dresser, the TV, the chair—all gone. Simone stepped in further, even the closet was empty.

She heard movement in the hallway. Just as she turned to find Zach, she saw Curtis standing in the doorway.

"Welcome back."

"Curtis," she said and her voice rose in panic. Then she turned back to her empty room. "All of my things—"

"Are in my apartment."

"*Excusez-moi? Pourquoi voudriez-vous faire?*"

Curtis took a step toward her and reached for her hands. "Whoa. You went home too long. I have no idea what you said."

Simone pursed her lips and focused on his eyes. Those damn blue, compassionate eyes. "Why did you do that?"

He ran his thumb gently over her knuckles. "I missed you."

"You did?" Her voice went up in pitch. She couldn't believe he was standing right before her.

He smiled and gave her a nod. "You look beautiful."

Simone looked down at her dress that gave to her swollen stomach. "Oh, Curtis." The tears were back. "I am sorry I did not tell you everything before."

Curtis raised his hand and rested it on her cheek. "Do you have something you'd like to tell me now?"

She looked down again and then back into those eyes that haunted her every thought. She rested her hands on her stomach. "I am pregnant with your baby."

The corners of his mouth softened. "I always wanted to be a father."

"Curtis."

"I love you, Simone."

The very words shook her to her core. "You do?"

He nodded and stepped to her until their bodies were pressed close. "I have loved you since we danced that first time. Do you remember that?"

His hand slid down her throat, over her shoulder, and down her arm until he captured her hand in his. With his other hand, he placed it on her hip and instinctively she raised her free hand to his chest.

Slowly he began to sway their bodies from side to side. The silent dance moved them closer together.

"Why did you move all my things?"

"Because I want you with me. I realized after you left that you shouldn't be the only one experiencing your pregnancy." He stopped the dance and gazed down at her. "I want to be a part of this."

Curtis' hands moved to the small mound of her stomach. When he touched her, she felt the life inside of her jolt, and he felt it too.

"Don't make me miss this, Simone."

All she could do was stifle her joyful sobs.

Curtis' hands came back to cradle her face. "Tell me I didn't move all this furniture for no reason, and tell me you'll live with me."

She nodded.

"Is that a yes?"

"*Oui.* I will live with you." The sobs subsided and a laugh escaped.

"Good, that bed is a pain in the ass to move. But not as hard as assembling a crib."

She sucked in a breath and fell into his arms. "You have a crib?"

"I want the woman I love and our baby at home with me, where they belong."

"I love you, Curtis. I am so sorry for everything."

He brushed her hair away from her face. "Promise me you will never leave me again."

"I promise."

"And promise me that we will be a family. You, me, and our baby."

She nodded in agreement.

"And it's up to you. We can get married now or wait until the baby is born."

Her heart was pounding in her chest so rapidly that she put her hand there to hold it in. "Are you asking me to marry you?"

"Very badly. But I want you to know it's because I love you and not because of our baby."

"You love me?"

"Yes."

She pulled him in as tightly as she could. "Say it again."

"I love you, Simone."

"I love you too, Curtis, and it would be a dream come true to be a Keller, no matter when."

There was a tapping on the door and they both looked up to see Zach standing in the doorway. "I take it this is all taken care of?"

"Yes, thank you for going to get her." He locked eyes with her. "She is my life." He placed his hands on her stomach again. "They are my life."

Simone held her breath. In that moment she knew any fantasy she'd ever had of making him love her had come true.

Zach dropped her suitcases in the doorway. "You two owe me for years."

He was gone before either of them noticed. "He's a good man."

She rested her head on his chest. "Yes he is."

"I'm glad he brought you into my life, and then back to me. I was lost without you and have been since you disappeared off that yacht."

Simone pulled back from him and looked down. "I have left everything to be here. My father disowned me and took his business away from Zach. My mother is horrified and embarrassed by me. I have nothing, Curtis."

"You're wrong, Simone." He brushed her cheek with his thumb. "You have everything right here in my arms." He rested his hands on her stomach again and the warmth from his touch resonated through her entire body.

"I thought it was a fairy tale, when opposites attract."

He chuckled. "You mean when the prince comes for Cinderella?"

"Something like that."

"Only you're the prince and…"

She shook her head feverously. "No. No." But the laughter broke free. "Okay, yes. Just like that."

"Fact of life, sweetheart. And trust me, this is more than attraction. This is forever."

"As in happily ever after?"

"Nothing less."

EPILOGUE

*N*ot only had Curtis moved her things into his place, he'd decorated the spare bedroom and created the perfect nursery.

"We are home, sweetheart," she said as she ran her hand over her stomach. "You are going to be very happy in this room."

She jumped when Curtis moved in behind her, wrapping his arms around her, resting his hands on her stomach.

"I was keeping it neutral. I didn't know if we were having a prince or a princess."

Simone rested her head on his shoulder. "I like surprises." She turned in his arms. "You were a surprise. The baby was a surprise. All of this," she sighed. "This is a surprise."

"Then I have one more for you." He kissed her gently. "Why don't you take a shower and get dressed. I have a new dress hanging in the bathroom for you."

She kissed him softly. "Are you taking me out?"

"Sort of. Just get ready."

Simone did as he'd asked, and an hour later she emerged in the beautiful dress Curtis had hanging up for her. She'd curled her hair, and put on makeup. She felt beautiful, even though her body was changing sizes by the minute, and she was exhausted.

Curtis sat on the sofa in a button up shirt, the sleeves rolled up to his elbows.

He stood when he saw her.

"You're radiant."

"Thank you," she said as she moved to him. "This is lovely."

"Regan picked it out."

"I thought she might have. My feet are too swollen to go into my shoes. I had to find a pair a sandals."

"My comment still holds. You're radiant."

Simone lifted her arms around his neck. "Where are you taking me?"

"You'll find out soon enough."

SIMONE WASN'T THE ONLY PERSON WHO LOVED SURPRISES. REGAN was quite fond of them as well.

When they pulled up in front of his parents' house, he wasn't sure she even noticed all the cars on the street.

"You brought me to your parents' house? Are we having dinner?" She asked? "I would have brought something."

"No need." He turned off the engine and opened the door. "Sit. I'll get your door."

He walked around the front of the truck, opened her door, and gave her a hand to help her out.

"You are being very suspicious," she laughed.

"Am I?" He pressed a kiss to her lips. "C'mon, let's go inside."

Hand in hand they walked up the front steps of his childhood home, and already he could hear the laughter from inside. Simone had heard it too.

When he pulled open the door, Regan rushed to her. "I'm so happy to see you," she said, planting a noisy kiss on her cheek and then taking her hand. "C'mon, we've all been waiting for you."

"For me? What is going on?" she asked as Regan pulled her into the living room where Curtis' family waited, Mary Ellen, and all of the girls from the clinic, including Cynthia—and a very uncomfortable looking Sam.

Curtis followed them, and when Simone turned to him, her eyes filled with tears, he smiled.

"What is all of this?" she asked as she brushed away the tears.

Regan wrapped her arm around Simone's shoulders. "This is your baby shower. Curtis is ill prepared for what is coming, and we wanted to honor you. Sit."

Regan shooed her nephew from the oversized chair and Simone sat down.

"Oh, this is a little overwhelming," she said brushing away tears.

Curtis moved in to sit on the arm of the chair. "You did say you liked surprises."

"I do. I love them," she admitted taking his hand and holding it in hers.

Regan handed her a wrapped box. "I'm glad you like surprises, and I know you love gifts. So let's open all of these, and then have cake. I'm starving for something sweet."

SIMONE LOOKED AROUND THE ROOM AT ALL OF THE FACES OF people she'd come to know and love. They smiled back at her.

She wasn't alone, and she'd never be alone again. She belonged to this community—to this family.

Curtis kissed the top of her head. "Are you okay?"

She looked up into those blue eye and smiled as she rested her hand on her belly. "I am. I've never been better."

"Before you open that box, I have one I'd like you to open."

Regan took back the box she had set on Simone's lap, and smiled at her brother.

Curtis stood from his perch on the arm of the chair and knelt down on one knee in front of Simone.

"I know you said you'd marry me already, but I wanted to make it official. And I wanted everyone we knew to hear you say it." He held a small ring box in his hand. When he opened it, a half-carat diamond ring sparkled back up at her. "Simone, will you marry me?"

The tears continued to stream down her cheeks, and she couldn't form words. All she could do was nod.

"I'm going to take that as a yes," he laughed as he slid the ring on her finger. "I promise to upgrade it when I can. I know you're used to more carats."

Simone clasped her hands around his hand and locked her gaze with his. "Never. That is a sweet gesture, but I am not who I was, and I am okay with that. That part of my life was not happy. And I am happy. Very happy."

"I promise to always make you happy," he said rising to place a kiss on her lips.

Resting his hand on her belly, she pressed her forehead to his. "As soon as I can fit in a dress, I am all yours," she teased.

"Oh, sweetheart, you're already all mine."

CENTER STAGE

CENTER STAGE

$\mathcal{A}$rianna pushed down on the suitcase and forced the zipper to close. The rest of her apartment was packed and ready for movers, but she'd need all her clothes before her belongings arrived in Tennessee.

She looked around her small New York apartment. It had been a good home to her for the past decade. She'd accomplished everything she'd wanted. When she'd moved there, it was to try her hand on the stages of Manhattan. She'd played in some dives and had worked her way up to leads on Broadway. She had a few commercials to her credit and had graced a few TV shows as an extra, but her love was still on stage. But now it was time to go home, back where her family was. Something would come together for her there. It always did.

Arianna looked at her watch. She had barely enough time to get to the airport. If there were any accidents backing up traffic, she'd miss her flight.

Her brother-in-law, Zach, had called and said her sister Regan had gone into labor with the couple's second baby. She figured she'd arrive just in time to get to hold the bundle of joy. Then, in a few more weeks, her brother Curtis and his fiancée Simone would have their first child. She knew moving back to Tennessee was the right move, and getting to spoil new nieces and nephews was reason enough to be closer to home.

THE FLIGHT HAD BEEN MISERABLE. LEAVING NEW YORK IN A January snowstorm always meant delays and aggravation. It was almost eight o'clock at night by the time the flight landed two hours late. Carlos would be livid if he'd been waiting at the airport the entire time.

She made it to baggage claim, retrieved her two pieces of luggage, and then scanned the area for her brother. There was no sign of him, or any member of her family, anywhere.

"I thought I'd missed you," the familiar voice behind her said.

She spun quickly to find John Forrester, Zach's most trusted building foreman, standing there.

"Missed me? Were you looking for me?"

"I have been sent to pick you up. Carlos and Madeline ended up with Tyler for the night."

Arianna narrowed her stare on him when he'd commented about her nephew. "I thought Mom was watching him while the baby was born."

"Well, it seems as though your family is going to grow quite a bit tonight. Regan is still in labor, and Curtis just took Simone in. She's having her baby today, too."

Arianna gasped. "Simone isn't due for two more weeks."

"Babies come when babies want to, and Emily thought she'd better be there for Simone." He picked up her suitcases, one in each hand. "C'mon, my truck isn't too far."

Who would have thought she'd get to be there for the birth of both babies in one night. God had blessed the Keller family—that was for sure. Carlos and Madeline's kids were teenagers, and in the next few years, they would be off on adventures of their own. Eduardo, their eldest, was already working for Zach after school.

Christian, their second son, was an all-star athlete—baseball, she thought. And Clara, well, Clara was a girl after her own heart. She was an accomplished musician on the acoustic guitar. And, boy, could that girl sing.

Regan and Zach's son, Tyler, was as anxious as any sixteen-month-old child could be for a new sibling. But Arianna figured he'd need the most spoiling from her to make everything just right.

As for her, she'd never wanted children. It just hadn't been in her plans. Her career had always been more important. She came and went as she wanted, carried on in any fashion she saw fit, and, of course, traveled the world.

But now, Nashville, Tennessee called her back home. Perhaps she could share her talent with the world in some other way.

John led her to his truck in the adjoining parking lot. She was comfortable with John, she thought, as she walked behind him. They had been each other's dates to both of Carlos' weddings the year before, and they had hit it off, as friends of course. They might have hit it off more, but he was very conscious of their age difference, even though she wasn't worried about the thirteen years between them. His ex-wife had burned him badly ten years ago, and it was clear he didn't trust any woman.

Not that she'd been looking for a man, but she often thought if John hadn't been so worried about everything, they might have had something. As it was, they could keep each other's company comfortably. Coming home with all her brothers and her sister being married, that might just be what she needed—someone to keep her company.

John's truck was probably one of the most beat up pickup trucks she'd ever had the displeasure of riding in, and she'd been born and raised in Tennessee—she knew bad pickup trucks. But that was John's character. If it still worked, there was no need to replace it.

He backed out of the parking lot and headed toward the

highway. Also common with John, he didn't have much to say unless you started the conversation.

"So, how is the construction business?" she asked.

"Zach keeps me busy. That's for sure."

"I'll bet. Do you think he'll take some time off after the baby is born?"

John laughed. "Sure he will. He'll work from his office at home."

Arianna followed suit and laughed too. That sounded like her brother-in-law.

She watched as John merged lanes. His tanned skin showed the many years that he'd worked in the elements. The deep lines around his eyes never made him look old, she thought, only distinguished. Arianna liked her men distinguished. Age on a man had never bothered her. Oh, if her parents knew about some of the men she'd dated in New York, they certainly might have had an opinion on the matter.

She must have been feeling the pang of needing someone to connect with, she decided, because the thought of running her fingers through John's salt and pepper shaded hair was almost irresistible. But she denied herself the pleasure. He probably wouldn't take too kindly to the lunatic sister-in-law of his boss making a move on him.

THE LONG FLIGHT AND DRIVE OUT TO THE HOSPITAL MUST HAVE worn Arianna out more than she'd thought. She woke to John's hand on her arm.

"We're here. If you hurry, you might not miss the show."

She rubbed her eyes. "Aren't you coming in?"

"Not my place to be. But I'll drop your bags off for you. I assume you're staying at your place?"

She nodded. It was one of the perks of keeping your house

when you moved away, especially if you knew you'd be back. "Yes. Of course."

"That was a sound business decision to keep the house and rent it out. Benson, Benson, and Hart keep good care of it."

"I wouldn't expect anything different. I know I have a renter in the basement, too. I hope they don't make too much noise. I'm a day sleeper."

John smiled. "Oh, he's a good guy. He won't bother you."

Arianna nodded and looked up at the hospital where her brother worked as an emergency room doctor. "Guess I'd better go meet the newest members of this crazy family." She slid across the seat and placed a kiss on John's unshaven cheek. "Thanks for the ride. I'll take you out for pizza and a beer."

"I never could turn down a woman who offered up pizza and beer."

She opened the door and climbed out. He was just her kind of man.

PLEASE RATE AND REVIEW

We hope you enjoyed *Opposite Attraction*
by Bernadette Marie.
If you did, we would ask that you please
rate and review this title.
Every review helps our authors.

Rate and Review: Opposite Attraction

ABOUT THE AUTHOR

Bestselling Author Bernadette Marie writes contemporary romances and believes in Happily Ever After. The married mother of five believes in love at first sight, quick love, and second chances. An avid martial artist, Bernadette Marie is a certified instructor and holds a second degree black belt in Tang Soo Do. She loves Tai Chi, traveling to Disney parks, and having lunch with friends. When not writing, or running her own publishing house, Bernadette is probably immersed in a Rom Com, from which she will often quote one-liners.

OTHER TITLES FROM

5 PRINCE PUBLISHING

www.5princebooks.com

Composing Laney *S.E. Reichert*
Firewall *Jessica Mehring*
Vampires of Atlantis *Courtney Davis*
Liz's Road Trip *Bernadette Marie*
Back to the 80s *S.E. Reichert & Kerrie Flanagan*
Granting Katelyn *S.E. Reichert*
Ghosts of Alda *Russell Archey*
The Serpent and the Firefly *Courtney Davis*
Raising Elle *S.E. Reichert*
Rom Com Movie Club No.3 *Bernadette Marie*
Rom Com Movie Club No.2 *Bernadette Marie*
Rom Com Movie Club No.1 *Bernadette Marie*
A Crossbow Christmas *Ann Swann*
Hot For Teacher *Felicia Carparelli*
The Happily Ever After Bookstore *Bernadette Marie*
Perfect Mrs Claus *Barbara Matteson*
Princess of Prias *Courtney Davis*
Paige and the Reluctant Artist *Darci Garcia*

www.ingramcontent.com/pod-product-compliance
Lightning Source LLC
Chambersburg PA
CBHW032143020726
47496CB00003B/689

* 9 7 8 1 6 3 1 1 2 0 2 2 0 *